*High Desert Angel*

Ava Wilson

# High Desert Angel

## Ava C. Wilson

CROOKED RIVER PUBLISHING
*Terrebonne, Oregon*

To order, visit our website www.avawilsonauthor.com

Printed in the United States of America at Gorham Printing, Centralia, WA

ISBN 978-0-615-96353-2

Dedicated to all of the brave women who served during WWII, and to my husband, Dan, who believes I can accomplish anything. I also owe a debt of gratitude to my children and grandchildren, who patiently read and critique copious versions of my writing. Their encouragement is what keeps me searching for another story to tell.

# CHAPTER I

IVY WAS UP BEFORE THE SUN BROKE over Green Mountain and the buttes to the east. In all her years in the valley, she loved waking up early; a cup of coffee on the porch, listening to ranch sounds, and scratching the dogs' ears made for a good start to her day. Later in the July afternoon, it would be too hot to sit on the porch in the direct sun; however, Ivy could retreat to the bench under the cottonwood trees by the spring, where it was cooler than even being inside the house. Her son always scolded her for not using the air conditioner, but Ivy stubbornly said she'd use it when he came to visit.

After a bowl of cold cereal and another cup of coffee, Ivy remembered that she'd had a visitor a day earlier. A woman from Portland drove all the way to Fort Rock to return an old photo album she'd found at a church rummage sale. It was full of Ivy's family pictures. Rosalie Evans, a book store owner, tracked down the family through clues in the old photos. The last Ivy knew of the album, her sister Lizzy had it at her home in Eugene. But Lizzy was gone, and so was their brother, Tom.

Ivy steadied herself with the cane as she retrieved the old photo album from the floor by her recliner. Seated at the kitchen table she began to thumb through the fragile pages. Ivy's floppy-eared old dog crawled under the table to lie across her feet, which satisfied both of them.

"Well, look at this, Biscuit, here's a picture of me, Tom, and Lizzy standing in front of the old school in Fort Rock," Ivy remarked to the dog, who cocked his head as if to hear better. The album had been filled by Ivy's mother, Martha Reese, with photos of their Oregon ranch during the Great Depression, and others sent by her children from faraway places. In one, Ivy's brother, Tom, looked sharp in his army uniform, with a girl on his arm enjoying a sightseeing cruise in Seattle's Puget Sound.

On the last page was a photo which was burned into Ivy's memory. She remembered well the day it was taken. Later she'd written a note about it, which was now taped below the photo.

> *By July of '44 my hair began falling out; malnutrition was our meanest enemy. I was never so hungry, even back in the hard days on the ranch. All of us looked angular, with jutting shoulder blades and bony hips. I sold another silver charm from my bracelet to buy some rice, dried mystery meat, and a few bananas, since the daily ration had been reduced again to about 700 calories. While chewing on a strip of dried meat, one of my teeth just fell out. My gums were so swollen that all my teeth were loose, so I had to be more careful after that. Mabel was no longer able to work, which meant she received less food. I was afraid that was the fate of us all. Our misery was compounded by the downpours that came every afternoon, turning the shacks into steaming boxes that the resident rats invaded to escape the torrents rushing down the paths. Every night, I wondered if I would ever see my lover again. My life in Fort Rock was just a faint memory.*

The grainy, black and white picture showed two women in wrinkled, baggy, and worn khaki clothing, standing among cots of sick or injured people who appeared to be located outdoors. Their thin faces reflected worry and hunger, and the forced smiles did nothing to hide that. The women squinted into insufferable sunlight, even though they were tucked under a tattered sheet strung above the cots. On the back of the photo, someone had written in pencil, "Ivy Reese and Mona McWhirter, May 1944."

Ivy heard David's pickup roll to a stop in the driveway. "Come on, Biscuit; let's go see what your buddy is up to today." When David stepped from the truck, Ivy thought to herself how much he resembled his father: his hair, smile, and the way he walked.

They met on the porch with Biscuit wriggling and wagging in excitement, even though he saw David almost every day. Ivy remarked that her son's hair was almost as white as hers, and he laughed at the often repeated observation. Of her three children, David was the one who stayed close, satisfied with a life of ranching in southern Oregon.

"I was just looking at the photos in that old album; want to join me?" Ivy asked.

He replied, "Only if you have some fresh coffee!"

Ivy took her time, explaining what was happening in each photo, and the more she talked, the more she remembered. David couldn't recall if he'd ever seen the photos, so he was full of questions. They poured over the album until lunchtime.

"Why don't you ride over to the house with me, and let Betty feed you?" he asked.

"Thanks, Hon, but I think I'll stay here. I'm enjoying looking at these old pictures, remembering the old days. My mother had such a hard life after Papa died. Before World War II she didn't have any conveniences; even water was scarce some years."

David listened closely to his mother's recollections because usually Ivy just talked about watching her children grow up on the ranch. His mother and dad had never disclosed much about their young lives in

Fort Rock Valley. It seemed that nothing existed before David and his sisters were born.

He said, "You know, Mom, I would like it very much if you'd write down all these stories about our grandparents, and you and Dad when you were growing up. I was wondering, why isn't there a picture of you two when you married?"

"I remember that a picture was taken by a friend, but it wasn't developed. I believe that the man who took it was killed a short time later," Ivy explained.

"Now you really have to write down everything!" David remarked with a questioning look.

Perhaps it was time to tell their story, while she could still remember.

# CHAPTER 2

TRACING MY FINGER ACROSS THE DUSTY WINDOW pane, I thought of all the house cleaning I could do if the well hadn't dried up. As if to emphasize the grip the drought had on southern Oregon in 1937, two large dust-devils zigzagged down the powdery road towards our wind-scoured house. Squeezing through the gate like two boys racing for home, the one-footed goliaths crashed into one another in a tall explosion of dirt, twigs and pebbles, which sent the chickens in the yard squawking and running under the porch. Already by May the temperature was stifling, and I felt sticky and badly in need of a real bath. Days were unbearably hot, but at least the nights cooled off after sunset. I couldn't stand the thought of spending another summer on the ranch, but had no chance to be anywhere else.

Up until he died, Grandpa Reese spent countless dusky evenings repeating stories about bringing his wife to the arid valley in 1895 where my father was born. At that time just a few ranches dotted the landscape, separated by miles across the high desert. For almost two decades rainfall was ample, providing an exceptional range of bunchgrass for raising cattle. Grandpa plowed some of his land, planting fruit trees and grasses. The cattle also grazed into the low hills surrounding the valley, just like all the other ranchers' herds using public land. What they didn't realize was that they were allowing the cattle to over-graze, from which the bunchgrass couldn't recover. As rainfall diminished over the years, Grandpa had to buy feed when his hay field produced less and less. He sadly watched the parched grass wither and grow sparse, allowing invasive weeds to encroach onto his hard-won land. The fruit trees died long before Ma and Papa married.

In 1915, when war was raging in Europe, Papa was nineteen years old, and met Ma at a barn dance in Silver Lake. Her folks had just moved to Eugene, across the Cascade Mountains, but she stayed behind to graduate from high school. Just three months later, they were married and moved into the old ranch house near Fort Rock with Papa's widowed father. Children came along quickly like they always did in those days.

About the time I was born, Papa hand drilled a shallow well by pounding a pipe, foot by foot, into the ground. Papa then built a windmill to pump the cold, sweet water for our garden and household, but it wasn't enough to irrigate a field of alfalfa. The Papa I remember was full of affection and jokes, although he expected all of his children to work for the success of the ranch. Papa suddenly died of pneumonia when I was six years old, leaving Ma with my two older brothers, me, and a baby sister. Ma worked alongside her father-in-law, trying to hold the ranch together, and when he passed away, she was left with the whole responsibility.

Ma wasn't alone in her struggle on the high desert since there were still several families nearby who were hanging onto the acres they'd committed their lives to improving. Most saw it as a way to have a legacy for their children; however, they hadn't counted on the Great Depression. If that weren't enough to discourage most farmers and ranchers, a drought of Biblical proportions smothered the country, leaving hopelessness in its wake.

Year by year our livelihood disintegrated. I can remember when we kids were young that asking for quarter to buy a friend's birthday gift didn't necessarily lead to a family conference. As I grew older, pennies and nickels were counted and saved, and we all looked for ways to earn a few cents. Little by little our herd diminished since the lack of rain turned our hay fields into barren stretches. A few wealthy ranchers drilled deep wells to irrigate fields of hay and fill water tanks for livestock. Their cattle fattened and calved with so much ease.

By 1936 our shallow well pumped only sporadically, and in another year, it dried up altogether. The windmill stood like a lone sentinel, silent as a dead tree. Ma had to sell our few remaining cattle and my horse, Pompey, to a Silver Lake rancher. The day Pompey was trailed off behind another horse and rider I ran into the house and wouldn't speak to Ma for the rest of that day. Later, I realized how difficult letting the livestock go was on Ma, too.

The Reese ranch had historically depended on rainfall and springs to fill the ponds for irrigation, so laboriously dug by Grandpa's family; but they became just bone-dry depressions dotting the landscape. I can barely remember the Sunday afternoons as a youngster, picnicking and swimming in the oval grassy-lined pond nearest the house.

From our house, dark buttes and thick forests could be seen to the southwest. To the east, flat sandy stretches were broken only by old lava flows, low scrub. and the occasional section-line road. Looking northwest, a crescent shaped remnant of volcanic activity eons earlier stood 300 feet above the desert. At a distance, it had the appearance of a stone fort, although there had never been a fort contained within the walls. Indians had used the structure before the white man came into the area and reminders of their civilization remained. Occasionally, a rancher would use the rocky enclosure during a round-up. A few temperamental springs and streams dotted the thousands of acres in the valley, but it was almost seventy miles in any direction to reach a respectable river. Small lakes and marshes came and went with the seasons and drought. Even as a child, I wondered why we stayed in Fort Rock. Other settlers moved on to more fertile lands, just over the Cascade Mountains or north toward the Columbia River. But why does anyone stay anywhere? Ma stubbornly maintained that the ranch must stay in the family.

Only Granny Ellen kept the family from starving-out during those hard years. She and Uncle Bob, Ma's only brother, raised a massive garden at their home in Eugene, on the wetter west side of Oregon. Each October their old truck limped over Willamette Pass with Granny, Bob, and his wife, Amy. They always stayed two weeks, during which time Uncle Bob and my brother Tom hunted elk, antelope, and mule deer. In the evenings Granny, Amy, and Ma pieced a quilt top together, which one of them would finish over the winter. I always found something to mend, just so I could sit near the lantern and listen to them talk over their sewing.

Usually Ma started out with some gossip about a neighbor, such as "Old Mr. Cooper is packin' up to move in with his son down in Klamath County. He says he's givin' this dry land back to the gov'ment."

"It'll rain agin, Martha, it's got to!" Granny would say. "But why don' you and the children come live with us 'till it does?"

Ma would patiently reply, "You remember, I promised both Robert and Grandpa Reese I'd hang on to the ranch at all cost, for Thomas to inherit." Granny Ellen had stopped asking about my other brother, Michael, who left home four years earlier when he turned seventeen. Michael was always getting into trouble around the valley, and balked at Ma's pleas to help Tom with the ranch work. She finally gave up and actually seemed relieved when he stole her egg money and left town while we were at church one Sunday. We heard from him one time, asking for Ma to bail him out of jail in Reno. It was heartbreaking for her, but she said she wouldn't take food out of our mouths just so he could get out of jail and get in more trouble. She liked to imagine that he eventually found a good woman who set him straight, and we'd hear from them one day.

Tom, the second born, helped keep the ranch afloat. From the time when we were just youngsters, I understood that he didn't want to be a rancher, but couldn't bring himself to tell Ma. Tom had heard all his life that the land had to stay in our family. After our cattle were sold, he obediently hired himself out, cutting fence posts in the forest for the big ranchers and doing some trapping in the winter. Tom came home two days a week to catch up on our own ranch chores. Ma, my twelve-year old sister Lizzy, and I sold eggs and butter to the general store, grubbed encroaching sagebrush from the pastures, kept coyotes away from the chickens, and waited for life to get better. Ma was proud that our ranch had never been mortgaged, so as long as the taxes were paid we were not in danger of losing it. Some years that tax money used what we squirreled away for clothes and shoes.

Many of the ranchers started with dugouts for homes, much like those used in the Southwest. Grandpa declared he wouldn't put his wife in the ground like a mole, so he built a plank cabin that was hotter in the summer and colder in the winter, than a dugout. He was proud of the windowed building, and over the years additions were added to accommodate the growing family. There was no insulation of course, but we kept the cracks stuffed with anything handy, and covered the inside walls with layers of muslin and wallpaper. My brothers usually slept in the small loft above the living area, except during the summer, when they took their mattresses out on the porch. After Grandpa passed away and Michael left, Tom moved into Grandpa's little room off the back of the cabin. We had no electricity then, so kerosene lanterns lit the house at night. It was a hard life, but I didn't resent Ma for staying on the ranch. That was her life, but it didn't have to be mine.

Life was about the same every day and school offered the only release from the drudgery of work on the ranch. The summer after I graduated from high school was a life-changer in so many ways. On an afternoon in May, 1937 events were set in motion that assured my life would never be the same.

I'd been working in the barn, cleaning up after the cow and putting feed in the trough. There wasn't good browse for Brownie in the pasture since the grass hardly came up before it was scorched and half covered with blowing dirt. I kept my hair braided and tucked under a sunbonnet to keep it as clean as possible, but my face was dusty and streaked with beads of sweat. Before opening the kitchen door, I shook my clothes to remove the dirt and hay twigs, and removed the bonnet so a splash of water could wash away part of the grime. A few minutes later I was daydreaming when the two dust devils burst into the yard, throwing more dirt into the air.

"Ivy, honey, git down to the cellar and find me a jar a' Granny's tomatoes," Ma called from the kitchen. "Boiled macaroni and tomatoes," I thought, and we were glad to have it. While many neighbors were eating nothing but brown beans, I smelled Ma's crispy cornbread baking in the oven. She had figured out that if we ate a quart jar of canned venison once a week, it would last until hunting season this year. There was so little moisture during those years, that most gardens withered before the flowers were pollinated, and 1937's weather was unbearably similar. For weeks, I carried buckets of water for the plants, from a dripping spring in some rocks by the pasture. Finally the dwindling trickle was designated just for our milk cow, Brownie. The only green thing we could keep alive was Ma's rhubarb plant… she called it her pie plant…that grew just outside the kitchen door. After dishes were washed each evening, the pan of water was carefully poured over the roots. Ma's rhubarb pies were legendary.

Since April of that year, we spent one dollar a week filling two wooden barrels with water from Ben Parley's deep well two miles away, which took care of bathing and cooking. Once a month, Tom hauled an additional barrel so Ma and I could wash all our clothes and bedding. Our flush toilet in the bathroom, which had been added on to the house just ten years earlier, wasn't usable after the well went dry. The old privy went back into service, after a little sprucing up.

"Tom's coming," Lizzy announced, seeing a dust cloud approach, as I set four places at the table. "Better set another place, 'cause he's got somebody with him." The two men were laughing when they got out of the rusty pickup. They stopped at the bench on the porch, sloshed water from the basin on their faces, and entered the kitchen, still laughing. It was good to see Tom enjoying himself.

"Ma, Ivy, Lizzy...this is Paul Mershom. Paul, these are the beautiful women in my life!" Everyone laughed, Lizzy blushed, and handshakes were given all around.

"It's nice to meet you, Paul. Are you from 'round here?" Ma asked, motioning for him to follow her to the kitchen.

"No, Mrs. Reese. I'm part of the CCC, uh, the Civil Conservation Corps, over at Cabin Lake. We're building forest roads from there up to Hampton," Paul answered.

"I got the truck high-centered on a boulder, and Paul's crew helped me out. I figured I owed him a home cooked meal," Tom laughed.

I looked so wilted, wearing my saddest skirt with Tom's castoff plaid shirt. Slipping into the curtained alcove which served as my bedroom, I undid my braids, brushed my long hair quickly, and tied a bright scarf around my head with the knot above my forehead. With my Sunday-best dress replacing the work clothes, I ran a damp cloth from the basin over my face and under my arms. All of this preparation took barely five minutes, but was noticed by Tom and Paul when I returned to the kitchen. Tom started to tease me about dressing up for company when Ma pulled me aside, whispering for me to fetch a quart jar of Granny's peaches from the cellar to stretch the meal. Tom showed Paul a large map on the parlor wall, pointing out the ranch in proximity to the Cabin Lake CCC Camp. Our guest appeared older than Tom, maybe twenty or twenty-two, and talked like he was well educated. I'd heard that most of the young men working for the CCC were recruited from job-starved towns and failed farms of the mid-west. Paul looked out of place in our shabby home, sporting a real haircut and work clothes that weren't frayed and stained.

Usually on the evenings when Tom was home, we listened to his crystal radio and shared tales of what happened during the week. Ma always maintained an air that our predicament was only temporary which made me wonder whether she was fooling herself, or just trying to keep everyone else's spirits up. That evening Paul added a fresh perspective to the drought, the country, and what young people were talking about. He had been at Cabin Lake only two months, having spent a year before that in Nebraska building a canal. Paul told us he was from Oklahoma and his parents were killed in a car accident.

"I sure do like the forested part of this country better than Oklahoma for sure," Paul said, and he proceeded to tell us all about the hardships back there. When the government men came around recruiting unmarried men under the age of twenty-five to work on roads, bridges, dams, and such, he said he jumped at the chance to work and get regular meals.

When I looked stealthily across the table to see Paul's even-toothed smile, I thought he was about the most beautiful man I'd ever met. He moved and spoke like a movie actor, sure of himself and totally charming.

I was so enraptured with Paul's discussion that I didn't hear the knock at the kitchen door. Tom whooped, "Hey Shorty, come on in!" Lee Johnson had been slow to get his growth spurt, and earned his nickname early. Although he stood almost six feet tall as a seventeen-year-old, the name stuck and I was the only person who called him Lee. Introductions were made all around until Lee remembered the reason for his visit.

"We're all going to Bend tomorrow for a few days and Mom says this pot of roast beef she cooked for the noon meal will go to waste if you don't take it off her hands," the young man awkwardly said.

"Tell Judith I appreciate that, Shorty, but now you've got to sit down and eat with us. I'll jest heat it up," Ma said.

Paul watched Lee maneuver a place at the table beside me, and I welcomed him as the old friend he was. Lizzy fetched another plate and fork and took her place on his other side. Everyone knew Lee considered me his girlfriend, and I'd often go riding with him across the buttes on one of his horses. Ma worried that I might pass up the chance to have a better life, as the wife of a successful rancher's son. I kept no secret that I planned to live in a city, far from cattle, dust, and weather worries. Lee and I were graduating from high school in a week; he knew he'd inherit his family's ranch, and was going to Oregon State College in Corvallis in the fall to study animal husbandry.

Paul asked me what I planned to do after graduating, and I told him about my dream of becoming a nurse. It was a dream I'd always had, but college the next fall was out of the question.

Tom was the jokester around the table, a role he loved to play. Paul and Lee fed into it, and the house filled with rollicking laughter. The evening was so full of antics that I forgot for a few hours the hard times which had cast a shadow over everything the last several years. Fort Rock was a close community, where families had been neighbors for a long time; however, many had given up on the valley.

The school was barely hanging on, and even in 1937 electricity and telephones were years away. The one general store was stocking less merchandise each year, so it seemed the valley was going backwards instead of developing into the lush and productive place the pioneers dreamed it would be. That evening the carefree group of friends and family gathered around the table did not dwell on the Depression, which had the nation short on cash and long on worries. Nor did we mention events which were out of our control.

About nine o'clock Lee finished drying the dishes for Lizzy, which he always did when he ate with us, earning a special place in her heart. He offered to take Paul back to the CCC barracks, since it wasn't too far beyond the Rocking J ranch. Paul was reluctant to end the evening but would get a reprimand if he came in much later. I strolled with the two young men across the dusty yard to Lee's truck; Paul thought everything I said was funny, but I knew he was just flirting. I also knew that Lee was annoyed that this stranger had encroached on his territory: me.

"I'll see you Saturday night at the grange dance, Ivy," Lee reminded me.

"You'll be back from Bend by then?" I asked.

"Yep," he said. "Mom wouldn't miss seeing her old friends from Thompson's Ranch. I guess a couple of trucks are bringing those folks, and they'll camp at our place afterwards. Want me to pick you up?"

I told Lee that Tom promised he'd be home in time to clean up, and get us there by seven o'clock, so I'd meet him there. I added, "I'm gonna bring angel food cake with chocolate frosting, so I know I'll see you."

Lee laughed as he walked around the back of his truck. Before he got to the driver's door, Paul quietly said from the passenger seat, "I might just have to sample that cake too!" And he winked at me in the twilight. I didn't know what to say, but smiled, and waved as the truck sped up the track. I stood in the desert darkness for a bit longer, watching the truck lights bounce along the road. The afternoon's wind had diminished so the air was clear, making it easy to pick out the Big Dipper in the pitch dark sky. Our hound, Sunny, stayed with me when I lingered on the porch. He wanted his ears scratched, and kept nudging my legs, so I finally obliged. Ma called for me to come on in since it was late, and she wouldn't go to bed until all of her children were safe in the house.

When Ma turned off the kitchen lantern, she drew aside the curtain of my bedroom to kiss me goodnight, and I asked her what she thought of Paul.

"I suppose he's nice," she answered, after a hesitation.

In the dark room, I couldn't see Ma's face, and said, "You don't sound convinced." I heard a match strike, and the candle on my dresser sputtered and caught.

Ma eased herself onto the edge of my narrow bed and asked, "What do you think?" I sat up, and Ma turned me aside and began braiding my hair. I winced when her chapped hands snagged on the tendrils. Ma worked as hard as any man every day, and I vowed silently again that I would never settle for a ranching life.

I answered Ma's question about Paul, "Well, he's awfully handsome, and different from the fellas I know."

"Well, he's older than most of the fellas you know well and that's part of why he's different," Ma added with a grin.

I could only reply that I thought he was interesting.

"Jest one thing I noticed," Ma said, "He don't talk like somebody from Oklahoma. Remember the Tate's from Tulsa? And Sawyer's from Ponca City? I could hardly understand their drawls."

"Probably won't see him again anyway," I said, and leaned up to plant a kiss on her cheek. Ma chuckled, "Sure."

# CHAPTER 3

ALL WEEK, EVERYTHING I PLANNED FOR THE dance was first measured by how Paul might like it. I knew Lee would like anything I wore or how my hair looked, but for some reason I wanted Paul to approve. I had listened to other girls complain about their figures, complexions and hair, and never understood why they cared so much. Now I wanted to look perfect, simply to seek approval from a man. Edith, my best friend in Fort Rock, always said I had the most perfect skin, while she fought blemishes all through high school. But Edith had a round, full figure, whereas I was thin, with a lanky build. Edith's hair was rusty red in color, short, and very curly, just like her mother's. On the other hand, mine was mousy brown, barely wavy, and was only cut a little each year. On the night of the dance Ma helped style my hair with the sides swept back to a barrette on my crown, and the rest tumbled below my shoulders.

For the first time in my life I had two fellows wanting all my attention, and more than just a few neighbors at the Grange dance noticed. I was a bit embarrassed as Lee cut in on Paul, and two minutes later the tables were turned. Each one complimented me until my cheeks burned; finally Tom had had enough and swept me away from the other two declaring, "I brought Ivy to the dance, so it's my turn and don't cut in!"

To be honest, I was relieved, since I didn't know how to handle such a situation. Lee was such a familiar part of my life; Paul, on the other hand, was a new, exotic, and mysterious interloper. Edith and I knew of other girls in Fort Rock and nearby Silver Lake who dated young men from the Cabin Lake CCC Camp; one couple had married and moved back to his home state.

At eleven o'clock Sheriff Newberry rang the dinner bell and announced that the food was spread on tables outside; a stampede of all ages made for the doors. Lee held back with me and I knew he wanted to talk while Paul joined a crowd of men from the camp.

Lee was quiet at first, and then surprised me by admitting, "For some reason, I dislike Paul calling me Shorty, more than anyone else I know." He reached for my hand, knowing I understood. "He's too smooth and makes me feel like a hayseed."

It pained me to realize Lee felt put-down by Paul, and I said as much. He shrugged it off, saying, "I can take it, but you shouldn't take him so seriously. He's had a lot of girlfriends, I hear."

"And just how do you know that?" I asked, rather defensively. Lee would only shake his head, and then said, "Me and Pop are going to Corvallis on Tuesday, might be gone nearly two weeks, buying some cattle and looking over the college campus. I could use a smile from my girl to take with me." We laughed, and he took my hand as we made our way to the food tables outside. Paul met us in the doorway and waylaid me with a plate of chicken, potato salad, beans and pickles.

"Hey, did you think I forgot you?" Paul joked. "I've got two forks, so we can share this big plate of food."

Lee said, "I'll get some and be right back, Ivy."

"Hey Shorty, it's my turn now. Come on, Ivy, let's find a quiet corner!" Paul smoothly insisted. Lee turned around and said, "I'll pick you up tomorrow about six, for the graduation ceremony, Ivy," and I just nodded. Paul and I talked about his job with the CCC, but he thought that most of the fellows were not interested in making something of themselves, like him. He claimed that college, nice cars, and lots of money were in his future, and I thought he sounded very sophisticated.

Ma and Lizzy went to church the next morning, while Tom and I listened to the crystal radio. The weather reports never changed for the better; just depressing news of more wind and dry conditions. Most of the stations the radio could pick up on Sundays were preachers shouting salvation or church music being played. He found a broadcast of band music and since Ma wasn't home, we danced on a Sunday morning in our shabby parlor, dreaming of ballrooms in our futures. Over the last of the coffee, my big brother told me of his real dreams to move away from Fort Rock Valley. The wind buffeting the old house emphasized Tom's reason for leaving.

"If I join the Army I can make more than working around here, and get trained for a trade too," he said, and I knew he'd been thinking of this for a long time.

"I'm just not interested in staying in the valley, Ivy. Do you blame me?" my big brother asked.

"You know I want to leave too, but it's easier for boys to get away," I complained. At that moment, the likelihood of my escaping Fort Rock seemed insurmountable.

In the end, he promised me he wouldn't do anything right away. I knew, and Tom knew, that he might not have the courage to disappoint our Ma.

Later that afternoon the wind let up, and Lee surprised me by showing up on Belle, his cutting horse, trailing Missy, his mother's favorite.

"Ma says Missy needs some exercise," he said, grinning.

We rode in the direction of Green Mountain, and stopped after awhile to water the horses and ourselves. The wind had tangled my hair, which I hadn't taken the time to braid; Lee cut several inches off his bootlace so I could tie it out of my face.

"Don't ever cut your hair, Ivy, or at least not very much," he said.

"I might decide to be a modern woman, and get a bob!" I teased, as we turned our horses back towards the ranch.

That evening our teachers, families, and friends were present for a brief ceremony, and the graduates (all four of us) exchanged gifts afterwards. Lee gave me a charm bracelet, with a tiny silver dog already attached. It was so thoughtful, but then that was Lee. He said he'd treasure the monogrammed handkerchiefs I made, embroidered with their ranch's brand. Ma handed me a little fabric covered box that contained a pretty ring with two rubies in gold filigree setting.

"Your Papa gave me this when you were born, and I think he'd want you to have it for your graduation present," Ma said, with tears in her eyes. I realized how much that ring meant to her and swore that I would take good care of it. Papa had been gone over ten years and Ma still missed him terribly. Holding onto the ranch was her attempt to hold onto him. I understood that their souls were wrapped together in this desolate land.

At dawn the next morning, a shotgun blast woke Lizzy and me. Ma caught a coyote slinking towards the chicken coop and promptly ended his reign of terror on our flock. Every two or three weeks Mother or Tom killed a varmint such as a coyote, rabbit, skunk, or snake. One thing I had to admit about living in Fort Rock Valley: life was monotonous, but never dull. Ma laughed at that, saying it didn't make sense, but I knew what I meant.

Monday was scorching, but we still had to heat water from the barrels to wash a huge amount of clothes. The copper boiler perched on an iron stand over a bonfire in the yard. Ma scrubbed on the rubboard in a wash tub that we kept filled with hot water, and Lizzy helped me wring, rinse, and wring again over the rinse tub. We'd run to the clothes line to hang things up, and in the heat the first pieces were dry by the time we'd hung the last of them. Ma rinsed the whites in bluing and starched what had to be ironed. These would dry on the line, then were sprinkled down, and rolled up tight in a cloth-lined basket. Washing was such a chore that we all wore our work clothes over and over. At the end of the week Tom's shirt could stand in a corner, supported by his dried salty sweat.

I didn't see Lee again before he left town. Somehow Paul managed to come to the ranch most evenings, hitchhiking to and from the CCC camp. Some days Tom would pick him up on the way home from the forest. Tom said Paul must have been sneaking away since the CCC boys were only free on weekends. Ma didn't like that, and called it "going AWOL." The first evening we played checkers until Lizzy begged to get out the new Monopoly game. When Tom was home, we played as teams with ruthless competition. One evening Paul asked if I would take a walk around the place before he had to leave. At first we sat on the old corral fence, and talked about everything from dreams of traveling to my life on the ranch. He said he admired folks who sacrificed comfort for wresting a livelihood from the land, but he had no desire to be a rancher or a farmer.

There was no moon that night so the stars stood out thick in the blackness, and Paul pointed out several constellations. He said that in the cities you couldn't see the wide band of our Milky Way because of the bright lights. I never thought about that and assumed everyone saw the same celestial wonders as I did. I remember thinking how smart Paul was and asked myself, "Will he be the one who takes me away from Fort Rock?" Paul said that he planned to become a businessman or a lawyer, and I was sure he'd succeed. I was infatuated with Paul, and he fed my ego with compliments.

On Saturday evening Paul convinced me to dance with him in the barn, while he hummed *Stardust* in my ear. His breath on my neck made me feel warm and happy. When the tune was finished, Paul kissed me lightly on the cheek. That night I couldn't sleep for wondering if I was in love. I became more convinced every evening that Paul loved me, and would ask me to leave with him one day soon. Things were happening so fast, but I had read enough books to know it could happen that way. Sunday morning Ma reminded me that Lee would return in a week and wouldn't be very happy that I had spent so much time with Paul.

"I don't belong to Lee, Ma!"

"You really don't know anythin' about Paul, Ivy," she gently replied.

I had to defend Paul, and said, "You don't understand. He makes me feel good about myself and besides, I'm in love with him!" She stepped back as if I had slapped her. I ran out the door with the milk bucket, glad to have Brownie as an excuse to escape Ma's eyes. Later, when I carried the bucket of milk into the kitchen, she turned from the sink and said, "Ivy, I'm goin' to Silver Lake for two or three days, and you and Lizzy are comin' with me. Tom can take care of Brownie and the chickens for us. If you'll get the butter churned, I'll bake a couple of cakes to take along. We'll leave in the mornin'."

"But…" I began.

"Tom can explain it to Paul; you can see him at the end of the week," she said with a finality I knew better than challenge. My Aunt Fay was Papa's oldest sister, the city clerk in Silver Lake, and a widow like Ma. Since Papa and Grandpa were gone, Ma always turned to Fay for help when she had a problem, unless she had time to write Granny. I knew the problem this time was me!

The road from Fort Rock to Silver Lake was a rutted and dusty twenty-mile track. Our old pickup had no springs left, so Ma drove as slow as a turtle, making the trip endlessly miserable. By the time we arrived, I felt like I had been dragged behind a plow all day. Aunt Fay didn't know we were coming but it didn't matter. Silver Lake had no electricity, but her house did have hot, running water, so we three enjoyed the luxury of long showers. In the evening, the two women sat in the porch swing, talking low and serious. I was in the parlor, reading a copy of Life Magazine, but could just make out what they were saying through the window screen.

"Oh Fay, sometimes I get so tired of keepin' the ranch goin'. The big decisions fall on me; but to be fair, the chil'ren are wonderful about workin' so hard and makin' do with bare necessities. If I didn't think there was an end to this drought, I couldn't keep goin'," I heard Ma say.

"Now Martha, neither Robert nor Pa would blame you for anything that happens. They had no idea times would get so hard for the country and especially small ranches out here," Aunt Fay said.

Only the sound of the squeaking swing came through the window for a few minutes, and finally Mother said, "I'm sorely worried 'bout Ivy. She's got herself infatuated with a fellow from the CCC camp. He's a smooth talker, and I'm afeared she's either goin' to run away with him, or be hurt when he up and leaves."

Fay said, "I'm not one to give advice … I never had a daughter, and was spared all of that drama! Oh … I don't mean to make light of it, I can tell you're worried. What about sending her to your mother in Eugene for a few weeks?"

"I would, but that might jest push her further away from me, and that's the last thing I want," I heard Ma say. I wanted to be angry with her, but I had to admit that although Paul wanted to hear about my family and life, I actually knew very little about him. Perhaps Ma was right.

The next morning I vowed to quit pouting about the trip to Silver

Lake, and hurried to the kitchen to help Ma put a big breakfast on the table before Fay left for work. The day became as hot as the kitchen oven, and while wearing as little as modesty would allow, we struggled to catch a breeze in the shade of the porch that afternoon.

Fay's daughter-in-law, Bonnie, dropped by to tell us that a medicine show was setting up for a performance that evening in the park. Ma asked Bonnie to trim her hair, and I thought she looked lovely in her newest house dress. Ma's hair was brown, with gray showing around her temples, but her skin wasn't as ravaged by the desert wind as some of her friends. Ma stood ram-rod straight and had a purposeful walk; she was really quite pretty.

After supper, we took a couple of blankets and settled on the grass to watch the flamboyantly dressed doctor (who Ma called a snake oil salesman) entertain the crowd with music and jokes. Blazing lanterns were strung around a truck embellished with starbursts and the face of a turbaned "swami" which gave the whole scene a mysterious atmosphere. Once the audience was softened up, he pitched his "Amazing Wonder Cure", a bottle of dark liquid that he claimed was a miracle cure for athlete's foot, female ailments, cancer, kidney problems, and dozens more health problems.

"And only four bits!" he exclaimed. None of our family was tempted and Fay said the elixir was described by a previous customer as a combination of castor oil and coal oil with hot pepper thrown in. The evening was actually a tonic for our moods and on the way home the next day Lizzy declared the whole visit as magical. In the following years, I recalled those days in Silver Lake as a time of sweet happiness.

The day we drove back to Fort Rock, the wind buffeted the truck all over the road. Dust in the air made breathing difficult, so the three of us kept damp cloths over our noses and mouths. Twice Ma drove off the road when she couldn't see the edge, but we managed to back out of the sagebrush. Sunny met us at the gate, gleefully barking to welcome us back home. Tom had left a note that he was working near Hampton that day. When he came back in the evening, we spent the next two hours rattling on about Silver Lake: hot showers, new friends, and the medicine show. Before bedtime Tom pulled me aside and said that Paul would come over the next evening. Then my big brother said, "Ivy, I guess Paul's an okay guy, but don't let this romance move too fast." Feeling very mature, I said I could take care of myself; however, when I remembered how Paul's touch felt when we danced, I wasn't so sure.

# CHAPTER 4

MY COUSIN'S WIFE, BONNIE, GAVE ME A dress to make over, so I started working on it right away. Edith and her cousin from Bend came to visit while I sewed and I told them a little about Paul. They giggled and teased me, but I was careful to let them assume it was nothing serious, because after all, it wasn't.

Paul came for dinner Thursday evening, and we put together a puzzle brought back from Silver Lake. He had arranged a ride back to Cabin Lake Camp with a co-worker, so at nine o'clock I walked him to the gate to wait. Paul complimented my new dress, saying I looked as smart as an office girl in the city. He nuzzled my neck, and presently I gave in to a kiss on the mouth, my first. Oh, the soft sensation of his lips on mine made me dizzy, and I swayed in Paul's embrace. One of his arms pulled my shoulders tightly toward him, and I felt the other slide into the small of my back. My insides were melting and my knees were like jelly. All too soon, his friend arrived and we reluctantly broke apart. Paul asked if we could get away from the ranch the next evening; he would try to borrow a car. I said I'd ask Ma if I could fix a picnic for us to take to Fort Rock Cave nearby.

Ma's forehead furrowed when I approached her about the picnic, and I just knew she would say "No."

Suddenly smiling, she said, "I guess that'd be ok, but you'll have to take Lizzy, of course."

Without thinking, I blurted, "Oh, do we have to?" In the end, it was agreed that Lizzy would come, and I started to plan what we'd eat.

I woke early, not able to sleep any longer. The desert was still cool and the sunrise over distant buttes exploded with purple, pink and orange streaks, fading as the sun rose higher. I loved early mornings like that, with the sun slowly stealing a peek over the hills before the golden disk moved fully above the valley. Early morning was the best time to heat the iron on the range, so I pressed a blouse and skirt and everything else in the ironing basket. Humming to myself, I didn't hear Ma come into the kitchen.

"Lizzy was sick in the night…has the cramps real bad," Ma said, as she set the coffee pot on the range. "You might as well plan on eatin' here this evening."

"Please, Ma," I begged.

Ma shook her head, "Not without someone else going."

I begged, "But there are always other people there. It's not like we'd be alone."

After a minute, Ma said, "Well, let me have my coffee 'n think on it."

I milked Brownie while Ma set dough for a batch of cinnamon rolls. In the afternoon I took the butter and four dozen eggs to sell to the general store, and used some of the money to buy a small bottle of hair shampoo. When I returned home, Ma told me to kill a chicken to fry for dinner.

"Why don't you fix a picnic to eat on the other side of the barn? Nobody will bother you, but you'll be close enough I won't worry. You could take Tom's radio out there."

It sounded silly, but it was the only way Paul and I could be alone.

After the chicken was fried and potato salad made, I heated a few pails of water and had a good soak. Ma and Lizzy used the same water to bathe, since we couldn't afford to waste so much. Usually we just bathed out of a pan, one limb at a time. When Paul arrived and heard what our plans were, he acted like it was a great idea and thanked Ma for fixing such a nice meal.

He ceremoniously ushered me to the car, and we drove to the back side of the barn. I spread the quilt over the sandy ground and Paul pulled a couple of hay bales out of the barn for us to sit against. The radio picked up some music from Los Angeles. We ate our chicken and potato salad and watched the moon rise opposite a pink sunset. When we finished, Paul motioned for me to move closer to him; I felt so safe in the arc of his arm behind my shoulders.

"Mmmm, you do smell nice," Paul said. His after-shave lotion had already made an impression on my senses. Paul definitely was nothing like the boys I knew around Fort Rock Valley.

"Paul, you've never said much about your family," I ventured. "Tell me about your life back in Oklahoma."

His forehead furrowed, as he asked, "Has somebody said something about my family, Ivy?"

I stammered, "Oh, no! I just wanted to know more about you," regretting that I had opened the subject.

Paul relaxed and said, "There's not much to tell, since my parents died when I was young. My aunt took care of me until I left home. What would you say about me taking you back there someday?"

"I think it would be wonderful!" I thought that surely he meant for us to marry, and honeymoon in Oklahoma.

We talked about my friends and family, the trip to Silver Lake, and laughed about the medicine show. He had been to a lot of those with his aunt, who even bought the potions being sold.

Suddenly, Paul said, "Ivy, you are so beautiful, you just don't know it" and we kissed, deeply and long. He pulled a flask from a pocket, took a sip and then held it to my lips. I hesitated, but at his urging

I finally allowed a few drops to trickle down my throat. At first it burned, and then I felt a warmness swarm through my body. Twilight had descended by then, and I felt like we were miles from anyone. One thing led to another, until I couldn't think for myself, especially after Paul professed his love for me. When I heard Lizzy call from the back door, I was surprised to find that we were inside the barn. My clothing was twisted around and buttons were undone. When I recalled what happened, I was on one hand, thrilled; however, the reality of our lovemaking horrified me. Reluctantly, we parted after I rode with Paul to the gate, and he promised to come back the next evening. Since he told me he felt so lucky to find me, I was certain he meant to have me for his wife.

After slipping into bed, I kept replaying over and over Paul's professions of love, and wondered what he was thinking right then.

Lizzy shook me awake at eight o'clock, chiding me for being "lazy bones." Ma left early in the morning with Tom, to take a cooked meal to a family near Christmas Valley who just welcomed a new baby. I washed myself, as if ridding the evidence of our lovemaking would remove the guilt from my mind. Lizzy had already milked Brownie so I dove right into housework. The memory of my evening with Paul was at once sharp and wonderful, while also hazy and confusing. One emotion I tried to push aside was the feeling of shame.

By the time Ma returned, I had scrubbed the floors and changed the sheets on her bed. Ma asked what we talked about for so long, and I told her what he said about his family. For supper we had bacon, gravy, and biscuits, but Paul didn't come after all. Tom was starting a new job the next day, driving for a logging company near La Pine and wouldn't be home very often. He left the pickup for us, and planned to hitchhike home every two or three weeks.

Lee came over the next day, and excitedly told us about the

campus in Corvallis and the courses he was taking in the fall. I was genuinely so proud of him, but could only think of announcing my news of getting married. I thought that if Paul would only come to the house, we might tell everyone in a day or two. Ma talked Lee into staying for supper, and I tried to join in on the banter around our table. Paul, once again, was absent. When I went to bed, Ma assured me that Paul had no control over what the CCC had him doing or where. She was sure he would show up in a day or so, but I knew she doubted Paul's sincerity.

Paul did not come to Fort Rock nor did I ever hear from him again. Two weeks later Tom returned from the logging camp. My brother seemed to avoid meeting my eyes, but with Lee and the family around, I couldn't ask him what the matter was. The date was July 1st, my birthday, and Lee gave me a charm shaped like a book for my bracelet. I hugged his neck for being so thoughtful.

"Well, I expected Paul to be here for your birthday, but it seems I don't have any competition tonight," Lee teased.

"I'm not sure what's going on at the camp," I replied defensively.

Tom cleared his throat, and muttered, "I rode part of the way home with one of the CCC engineers, and he said Paul is gone." We all waited speechless, until Tom sighed, and then said, "Seems like they found out he is married, so he's been shipped home. He wasn't from Oklahoma either."

The rest of the evening was a blur.

# CHAPTER 5

AT NO OTHER TIME IN MY LIFE was I ever so ashamed. I was no better than the loose girls I heard women whisper about. I couldn't even expect Paul to marry me to make things right. I tried to keep myself together because I couldn't stand for Ma to be disappointed in me. Finally, she flat out asked after one of my moody days. I couldn't lie, and cried like a baby in her arms. She never got angry with me; in fact Ma blamed herself for trusting him too much when she felt something wasn't right about him.

"We have to be thankful that you weren't 'caught,'" Ma said, since she knew I was having my monthly.

I avoided going anywhere because I had the feeling everyone was looking at me. Ma and I talked late at night, mostly worried whether Paul told anyone about our tryst. My mistake should not become Lizzy's cross to bear, and I knew how cruel folks could be about a thing like this. Lee came around often, but I wasn't very good company for him. I had disappointed myself so deeply; I felt my worth was rock bottom. Lee could never know that the girl next door was a fallen woman. Day by day life crawled on in the valley, and I held my breath against someone divulging my secret, a secret to keep forever.

Fort Rock Valley was sizzling in the July heat, baking anything once green into brown, lifeless twigs. When we thought it couldn't get any worse, the wind gathered up the blanket of topsoil and moved it into Idaho. All across the high desert, rivers shrank into streams, streams became small creeks, and creeks soon dried up. As bad as I felt when looking at the valley's sad condition, the older generation was devastated as they watched decades of hard work become sterile and silent. We heard of a man near Hampton who went berserk when the bank sent him a foreclosure notice. He shot his wife and then himself. I was depressed with my own failure, and the news around the valley added to my morose mood.

Ma decided she had to think of a way to send me to a nursing school. She sent for Aunt Fay, who drove up to the ranch Friday evening. Fay and Ma talked late into the night and hatched a plan. A letter was sent to Papa's Aunt Matilda in Portland. I hadn't seen her in several years, but I knew Ma wrote her often. We received a letter back quickly; she offered to pay my tuition for nursing school, if I could live with Granny while attending the university in Eugene. All I had to do was waste no time completing the application forms and hope to be accepted. My Fort Rock teachers responded quickly with letters of recommendation, and with my good grades, Aunt Fay thought I had a very good chance of being accepted to the program. Ma wrote Granny Ellen about my plan, and her reply was, "I've got my fingers crossed!"

I got a job waiting tables in the Fort Rock Café, from six a.m. until after lunch, as my first job working for someone besides family. After my application was completed and mailed, the weeks dragged by while I waited to hear back from the university. Lee came to the house almost every evening to get the latest news, and I felt that he wanted my chance for college as much as I did. Finally at the end of the third week of August a fat envelope arrived from the university's registrar. I left it unopened until the whole family was together in the evening, and Lee had arrived.

"The University of Oregon is pleased to inform you ...," it began. And before I could say another word, the room erupted into chaos! Tom picked me up and swung me around and around! When he finally stopped, Ma and Lizzy crushed me with hugs, and then Lee took my hands and danced us across the room. "I'm just so proud!" Lee burst out. Everyone else laughed, "Me, too!" Finally, I read aloud the whole letter, and looked over the other documents which held instructions for completing the process. To help pay for some extra fees associated with the nursing program, I was given the opportunity to work a few hours a week cleaning floors in the science building. I could only think of one thing: my cup runneth over! I owed so many people for making this happen.

Later in the evening when Ma and I were alone, I asked her what she had written to Aunt Matilda.

"I told her how much you had dreamed of being a nurse, and I thought your Pa would've wanted you to have a good education and career. She didn't hesitate a'tall when Fay and I asked for her help; in fact, she didn't understan' why we hadn't mentioned nursing school for you months earlier."

"I'll write her tomorrow about the acceptance letter, and thank her properly! She'll never know how much this means to me," I said through tears. "And I'll write Granny to let her know she'll have a roommate in a few weeks."

Ma said, "Shorty ... oh, I guess it's time I call him Lee ... well, he is so proud of you!"

"I know Ma, and I don't want Lee to ever know what happened between me and Paul."

"Jest let him be your friend for now, Ivy. He's a mighty fine young man," Ma advised, and I knew she still had hopes we would be together one day.

"It wouldn't be fair to Lee to be any more than friends, Ma. He deserves a nice girl without skeletons in her closet."

"Ivy, along your whole life, you'll come to what I call crossroads. You take one road an' you have one kind of life; another road leads to somethin' entirely different. This happens many times in a life, and once a choice is made to go left or right, it can't be done over. You just have to make the best of the road you took. This is your first grown-up crossroad."

Surprised at Ma's insight, I suddenly appreciated her more than ever; however, I didn't realize at the time how much comfort those words would bring in the future.

I had only two weeks before reporting to the university and spent the time working at the cafe and sewing some new clothes. Aunt Fay and Bonnie came up from Silver Lake one weekend, bringing fabric and patterns for two new dresses. Even Lizzy added to the assembly line by hemming each item. My café tips helped cover last minute purchases and other expenses.

Lee's visits were infrequent the last week at home, and when he did come by, he was quieter than usual. He never mentioned my infatuation with Paul, and silently I thanked him for that. One afternoon, Lee came to fetch me for dinner with his family.

"It's a special request from Mom," he said. "She says you can't just up and leave without seeing her."

I washed up and changed into a white pique dress that Bonnie made over for me. Over the summer I had learned how to plait my long hair into a French braid and when I stepped from behind my bedroom curtain, Lee whistled, long and low.

"Wow, Ivy, you're a knockout!" he said, and when he saw I wore the charm bracelet, he grinned.

On the drive to their ranch Lee told me that he was taking his pickup to school in Corvallis, and could drop me off at Granny Ellen's on the way. It would save Tom from taking off work to get me to Eugene.

"Are you coming home for Thanksgiving?" he asked.

"No, Fay asked me to join her at Aunt Matilda's for a couple of those days, and I really should since she's the reason I'm even going to college. But I'll be home during the Christmas holidays."

Lee responded, "Me too. Maybe I'll drive down to see you in Eugene before then. Is that okay?"

"Silly," I said, "of course it's okay. I'll be interested to hear if you like your classes. I'm kind of nervous. Are you?"

"I hadn't really thought about it that way. If the classes are too hard, I will be more than nervous!" he laughed.

As we approached the Rocking J's gate Lee pulled to the side of the road and said, "I'm really glad you came tonight, Ivy. Mom has been kind of down in the dumps with the drought and wind and ranch stuff. I think my leaving for college just now is bad timing."

It was easy to see that Lee was worried about his Mom, but I just agreed that the weather had everyone depressed, and while my Ma was excited about my opportunity in nursing school, she also kept hugging me for no reason at all.

From the first moment in Mrs. Johnson's kitchen, I understood what Lee meant. She was fidgety and talkative one minute, then would stare out the window over the sink, lost in thought. I helped her by setting the table, and tried to engage her in conversation. Their new ranch house was immense, full of stylish furniture purchased in Portland, and looked like homes I'd seen in magazines. Lee's grandfather bought their land in 1915 from an early settler, and the next generation continued to add improvements. Every year Mr. Johnson improved the pedigree of his herd, and usually bought the newest farming equipment for the hay fields. In 1935 they hired a contractor from Portland to build the fancy ranch house. It was wired for electric lights, which lit the house beautifully when Lee started the gasoline generator. Ma, who never said anything bad about her neighbors, commented once that she didn't know how they could sustain such expenses with beef prices so low.

Lee's parents were strangely quiet at the dinner table, which seemed odd since I had been asked to come. When I helped Mrs. Johnson clear the dishes, she surprised me by taking my hands in hers.

"I'm so happy you came tonight. We're very proud of you, Ivy," she said. I was so touched by her emotion.

I linked my arm with hers and said, "And I am so proud of Lee. He's always known that he wanted to be a rancher, just like his dad. Lee's the one who always encouraged me to think about a university degree."

"Ivy. You know him better than anyone else; let me know if he is homesick or needs something," she said.

"Of course I will!"

Lee poked his head around the door, and asked if I were ready to go home, since he knew I had to be at the café so early the next morning. On the way home, Lee confided that he suspected the Rocking J Ranch was having money problems, but he couldn't get his dad to discuss it with him. He told his parents a day earlier that he wanted to put off college for a year, and they both said he was not going to change his plans, everything was fine.

At the screen door Lee reached out to touch my bracelet, and said, "You need a few more charms on here." His touch was comforting and familiar, and I said, "I like it just as it is." Before leaving, he pecked me on the cheek, which made me feel like a Judas. I couldn't let him be fooled into thinking I was the same girl as the one at the Grange dance; but I couldn't tell him the truth.

# CHAPTER 6

DURING THE FIRST COUPLE OF MONTHS IN Eugene, the crush of strangers on the streets and campus overwhelmed me. I soon learned to ignore the distractions beyond my immediate bubble. It wasn't like I was ignorant of activity in a crowd, but it didn't impact my concentration as much as it could have. When I described this to Lee, he called it my survival instinct. We agreed that rural living has its good side, but it doesn't prepare a person for the cities.

Granny Ellen's home was a welcome sanctuary each evening and weekend, and for the first semester I seldom left except for school or errands. Uncle Bob and Amy lived on the back part of Granny's property in a tiny cottage, but the main residence was large, and was once used as a boarding house. The main floor of the old house shined with its old glass accents and mahogany woodwork and held a modernized kitchen, parlor, dining room, Granny's bedroom, and bath. The second floor held two bedrooms and a bathroom that was serviceable. Also on that floor and the one at the top of the stairs were several more rooms and bathrooms which needed numerous repairs. My bedroom was as big as the parlor back home. Although I remembered the house from our last visit five years earlier, I never dreamed I'd be living under that roof.

For the first time in my life I was surrounded by many young people who were bent on improving themselves. Although other classmates were also from rural areas of Oregon, not many lived without electricity or telephones. I began to feel like a hayseed with my homemade clothes and countrified speech. I wanted to fit in, so I watched and listened to the other young women.

My first semester was all classroom instruction which included psychology, English, nutrition, and math. The nursing school students were taught these classes as a group, not assimilated into the general university courses, so I met few people outside my field of study. I noticed a division of socialization between the students: those from families who came west two or three generations earlier were considered "real" Oregonians. Recent arrivals from other states were subjected to a snobbishness that appalled me. Of course, I had a long history of pioneering ancestors, but still didn't understand the pervasive attitude held against new residents. Right away I made friends with Mona McWhirter, a twenty-four year old from an Idaho Irish family. Mona had spent eight years working as a companion to a handicapped girl, and saved her money for college. She wanted nothing more than to be a nurse, and I felt guilty that my way was made easier than hers. One thing was curious about Mona: I knew she came from a poor family because she had taken care of herself for years; however, her speech and mannerisms were more refined than most other students. One evening I asked if her family was educated.

"Oye! Faith and begorrah!" Mona exclaimed, slipping into her Mother's tongue. "My home was far from that! Until about 5 years ago, I spoke like my parents with an Irish brogue so thick you wouldn't have understood me at all. When I was hired by Mr. Anderson to work in the big house, a whole world blossomed in front of me. Annabelle, who had polio and was in a wheelchair, was a year older than me. I was hired to accompany and entertain her; however, she became a dear friend, and taught me to speak and behave like a proper lady. She encouraged me to pursue my dream of college and a career."

I asked, "Could you help me speak better? I've been working on not using 'ain't' but that's not enough. I'm not dumb, Mona, but I think I'm judged by how I sound, not what I know." My sweet new friend said she'd love to help me, just as she was helped. We forged a tight friendship from that moment.

During the time I stayed with Granny, I was expected to do chores on the weekends, and I wouldn't have had it any other way. We canned hundreds of jars of fruits and vegetables. Some were bartered at the shoemaker's shop and some for auto repair, but most were taken to Fort Rock or used right at home. I did all of Granny's ironing, using her amazing electric iron. Having electricity made me realize just how difficult life was on the ranch, and I wondered at Ma's dogged determination to stay there. The telephone was something I had no trouble learning to use. Lee gradually got into the habit of calling me once a week. If only I could've called Ma and Lizzy, I wouldn't have missed them so much. I had never been away from home more than a night or two and I missed Ma's soothing assurance that everything would be alright. Ma and I had agreed to write each other every Sunday evening. I watched for the familiar envelope that arrived every Thursday or Friday; in about half of the envelopes Lizzy or Tom included a note. One of my biggest regrets about being so far away was Lizzy's growing up without me. Edith and I wrote occasionally and I depended on her to tell me what my old classmates were doing. When Granny, Bob, and Amy left to take the cases of canned food to Ma, I wanted to jump in the back of the truck and stowaway to Fort Rock.

Each day I awoke in great anticipation of the knowledge placed in my path. My brain was a sponge, absorbing facts and figures until I felt my head would burst by the end of the day. Math was the greatest stumbling block for both me and Mona. She had just spent a year working with a tutor completing high school prerequisites for the nursing program, but couldn't afford to pay for any more help. Lee came to our aid one weekend in October and spent hours explaining algebraic formulas, with hints on how to memorize the material. I'm certain that if he hadn't rescued me, I might have had a very short college experience.

Thanksgiving's holiday trip to Great-Aunt Matilda's home with Fay was relaxing and amazing at the same time. She was quite elderly, older than Granny Ellen, but still sharp-minded and kept telling me how proud she was that I had chosen a nursing career. Her late husband had owned a lumber mill and they had no children. She lived modestly in an ivy covered house near downtown Portland.

Portland is an easy city to love, with shade trees, riverfront parks, and elegant buildings. I felt a bit guilty for such a wonderful holiday, remembering how hard Mother worked, only to have bare ground instead of lawn, sage brush instead of flowers, and no real conveniences. I wanted to understand why Mother held onto the ranch in that desolate country, but it would be many years before it was clear.

Aunt Fay took charge of preparing Thanksgiving dinner, with assistance from me and Aunt Matilda. Two distant relatives I'd never met came for dinner; the two women about Ma's age were rather quiet, except to disapprove of a nursing career for a "lady." Later, Fay told me they were old maids who were bitter that life had passed them by, but did nothing to alter their situations.

When I returned to Eugene, classes became almost frenzied, with final papers due and daily testing. I cleaned the science building's floors at five a.m. so Mona and I had evenings free to drill each other for the next day's test. I was so excited about going home for

Christmas vacation, but regretted that Mona could not return to Idaho. She landed a job for the holidays at the hospital, washing dishes and mopping floors. Granny suggested that Mona give up her rented room and move in with us, which caused quite a celebration in the house. The arrangement was a boon to Mona's finances, since Granny only charged her a nominal fee for food, but nothing for the room. To repay this kindness, Mona took on the regular chore of washing windows and scrubbing all the floors each week. Uncle Bob and Amy considered Mona part of the family, as I knew they would. At that time, my dear friend and I had no idea how intertwined our lives would be for years to come.

Lee picked me up the first morning of the Christmas vacation, thinking we'd be in Fort Rock by nightfall. A sign on the highway heading east warned that Willamette Pass was closed due to heavy snow, so Lee drove us north to connect with the road over Santium Pass, which was better maintained, with heavier traffic. We talked non-stop across the mountains and valleys, tripping over each other's words, laughing for miles. By the time we reached Bend, fat snow-flakes were plopping rapidly on the road so we decided to stay the night with Lee's aunt and uncle. They were very sweet, still called Lee "Shorty" and were happy we stopped over with them. From the conversation at the dinner table, it was clear that Lee had told them all about me and nursing school.

I remember like it was yesterday, sitting on the carpet in front of their huge fireplace after dinner, dreamily watching the flames. Lee and I were the only ones still awake, but not many words passed between us.

"I'm really proud of you, Ivy," Lee finally said. "Are you happy?"

I was surprised at his quick question, and realized that even I hadn't asked myself that after Paul's lies were disclosed.

"Who wouldn't be happy with getting to do what I've dreamed of for so long?"

"I was worried about you after Paul left," Lee shyly responded. "You seemed so sad and I only want you to be happy... can't think of anything else." I remember looking at my young friend, as if seeing him for the first time. Lee was so earnest and true-blue, and I realized that I did love him. How could I have allowed a stranger in our valley get between us? It wasn't just that Lee was smart and kind. I'd always been attracted to how handsome he looked in his Levis and pearl-button shirts! Undeniably, my heartstrings were tugged by the look in his eyes, the shape of his mouth, and the feel of his touch. In that moment I couldn't dismiss the warmth I felt with his closeness; but my own foolishness had convinced me I didn't deserve Lee.

I touched his hand on the floor, and said, "I am happy, Lee, I am." I felt so much older than Lee at that moment. I wondered if I would ever forget the events of that summer. Could I pretend that it happened to some other girl, or would I awake every day and remember the moment of betrayal?

Both Lee and I were anxious to get home and left Bend at daylight. The snowy roads slowed our progress all the way south to La Pine; when we turned southeast the weather was more kind, with only traces of snow once we passed Moffitt Butte. Oh, the desert smelled so good, even in the cold winter temperatures. Crisp, clean, quiet... especially quiet!

Ma must have been hanging by the window all morning watching for us, anxious since we did not arrive the day before. The house smelled of cinnamon and it was plain that Ma had rolls in the oven. Lee stayed awhile, answering all of Tom's questions and grinned when Lizzy asked him to sit at the table by her while Ma served up warm cinnamon rolls. Finally, he had to leave, assuring me he'd be back over in a day or so for a proper visit with everyone.

The house seemed very small after living in Eugene. Tom had painted the kitchen walls and cabinets, which brightened the room considerably. I felt that Ma was afraid I would be judgmental after city life, so I was careful to tell her how wonderful it was to be back in my own home. Lizzy hung onto my every word, and asked if she could sleep in the bedroom with me that first night. She made a list of all we would do while I was home, which included the Grange Christmas Dance and the New Year's Eve party at Lee's house.

Edith came over the next day, and by that evening we had dozens of cookies ready for the holidays. Sandwich cookies with butter crème filling were my favorite to make; Lizzy rolled and cut out Christmas tree shapes that we decorated with green sugar sprinkles. Ma always made Russian tea cakes rolled in powdered sugar, and Edith chose chocolate drops. Ma already had two fruit cakes wrapped in rum-soaked cheesecloth sitting in the cupboard. Granny sent me back home with two cracker tins full of fudge squares, and several jars of mince meat for pies. Edith left before dark, carrying a tin filled with samples of the treats for her family.

The weather turned very cold just prior to the Grange dance, but the building's big potbelly stove was blazing when we arrived. A three-piece band played all of our favorite dance tunes and we laughed through several sing-along pieces. Lee was a fantastic dancer, and especially liked swing and the Lindy, so he danced my feet off! I was so proud to be seen with him, and have folks ask about our college classes. The last dance tune played was *As Time Goes By*, and I felt Lee's hand tighten around mine. Tears sprang in my eyes, which he noticed. I brushed them away quickly as he asked, "What's wrong, Ivy?"

I shook my head, "Nothing, silly, just sentimental about being home I guess…and so happy to be here with you."

"Now, that's what I like to hear!" he laughed, and dipped me low as the music ended.

When he took me home it was too cold to sit in the truck, so we tip-toed into the parlor to exchange presents. Lee bragged on the mittens I knitted with Granny's help. She showed me how to sew leather across the palms for a better grip, which was what he liked the best. When I opened the little box Lee handed to me, I saw the most beautiful charm nestled in crushed velvet. It was silver, of course, but this one had two tiny hearts in a filigree design linked together, with a little diamond placed precisely where they joined.

"Lee, this is too much! I love it, but you shouldn't have!"

"I want to, Ivy. You're my girl, right?" he asked. I smiled and nodded. We shyly embraced, and then he left. I sat in the parlor for a long time, thinking how good I felt at that moment.

Tom came home for Christmas, but had to return to work after two days. Right after he left, snow began falling like feathers dumped from a torn pillow, depositing two feet of snow on the level, and drifts that blocked most roads. The first couple of days I was content being trapped indoors, but when we heard a commotion in the yard and saw Lee pull up in his old horse-drawn sleigh, Lizzy and I gathered our coats, hats, and gloves and met him at the door. For as long as the snow lasted, a sleigh ride was a daily affair; however, by New Year's Eve, warmer weather and winds scoured the hills until they were just brown and muddy humps.

Mr. Johnson was still in Bend on business New Year's Eve, so Mrs. Johnson asked Ma and me to help get the house decorated. She'd hired a band from Lakeview, who billed themselves as "sounds of Glenn Miller." I think our mothers enjoyed the evening as much as the young people. In my opinion, the band sounded just like the music on Tom's radio, broadcasting from a New York ballroom. A few minutes before midnight, Lee pulled me into the kitchen, away from the crowd. When we heard everyone yell "Happy New Year" Lee nervously kissed me softly, sweetly. My only regret was that I hadn't waited for him to be the first. Edith burst into the room, laughing, "So here you are!" We joined the party, ate eggs, hotcakes, and sausage at one in the morning, and then everyone drifted home.

All of the family, except for Tom, spent a few days in Silver Lake with Aunt Fay. There was talk that Fort Rock School was going to close at the end of that school year since so many families had moved away. I overheard Ma and Fay talking about Michael, wondering where he was and if he was okay. As the years went by, the trouble he caused as a youngster faded and Ma longed to see him again.

By the time the holidays were over, I was ready to return to Eugene, especially to find out what my grades were. On our drive over the Cascades, Lee told me that his Dad was trying to sell off some of his pedigreed cattle, to help pay for the equipment he purchased the previous summer. Lee was worried, and so was I.

# CHAPTER 7

MONA AND I CELEBRATED OUR FIRST TERM'S grades; our hours of studying and quizzing each other paid off with grades we were proud of. By this time I was confident I could successfully do what it took to be a nurse, and I loved the work.

In April, Lee visited us for a weekend, and told me his heartbreaking news: his father had lost the Rocking J ranch. Lee learned that Mr. Johnson had borrowed too many times against the ranch to cover operating expenses. Their new home, new furnishings, new equipment and cattle had all been purchased with borrowed money. He had fought the foreclosure all winter, keeping most of it a secret from his wife and son until the sheriff came to the house with the court papers. Lee's mother had suspected something was wrong, and after her husband admitted his deceit, she had a nervous breakdown. Following treatment in the Bend hospital, she moved in with her sister there. Mr. Johnson was in Portland, looking for a job to support them. Lee couldn't understand why his father kept spending money that they didn't have. When Lee's father inherited the ranch, it was free and clear of any mortgage or debt. Lee was lost: all of his plans for the future hinged on the land and livestock. When he managed to get details from his father, it appeared that the new house was the last straw, tilting the ranch into unrecoverable financial ruin.

Lee told me, "I think Dad wanted to keep up the illusion he was successful, the most important rancher in Fort Rock Valley." For years Lee had a dream to continue the legacy left by his grandfather. Not only was the ranch gone, he couldn't even afford to continue college the next year.

By June, our first year of schooling was over, having completed more courses in psychology, English, math and nutrition, as well as an introduction to nursing practices. For the summer term each student was assigned to a ward in Eugene's hospital for six weeks, but I looked forward to going home for awhile first. As funny as it sounds, I craved the warmer, drier weather, since all winter long the Willamette Valley had nothing but rain, rain, and more rain. Too bad some of it didn't get over the Cascade Mountains to help the desert ranches.

Lee drove us to Bend where his mother lived. We had arranged for Tom to meet us at a park, so the three of us could talk. Lee asked Tom what he thought about joining the Army, and Tom's face broke out in a big smile.

"Shorty, you must be reading my mind! I've been watching what's going on in Europe, and think we might be in a war before long. I'd like to get a head start, and maybe make something of myself," Tom said.

"I need to make a living since more college is out of the question right now," Lee replied. "A couple of classmates are joining up this summer, and it got me to thinking."

I knew Tom had considered going into the army, but Lee caught me unaware. He was so young, just eighteen.

"Don't you both think you should wait awhile? Uncle Bob isn't so sure we'll be drawn into war," I pleaded to both of them. "And Mother will have a fit." The radio reported every day about Germany's invasions and threats to all of Europe. Our government seemed hesitant to enter the fray, other than selling weapons to our friends.

Tom said, "Ivy, even if we don't go to war, the U.S. is going to beef up the military forces, and I can be trained to do something useful. Hauling logs isn't what I want to do forever."

"He's right," Lee interjected. "Things are going to change soon, according to the buzz around campus."

"How will you break the news to Ma?" I asked Tom.

"I'll have an allotment sent to her, which will help keep our heads above water with ranch expenses. There's a rumor that the logging company will lay off truckers this fall, so we'll be struggling again to pay the taxes."

I could see that Tom had thought long and hard about this decision, and he was tense just mentioning it to me.

Lee said, "Do everything you can to keep the ranch, Tom. I wish I had that option."

Tom clapped Lee on the shoulder, "I'm real sorry about your place, Shorty. Don't be too hard on your dad; sometimes we just get caught up in something, and pretty soon it's out of control. You can't fix this but try not to dwell on it, or it'll eat you up."

His comment caused me to suspect that Ma had talked to Tom about the crossroads in our lives. She certainly would've been pleased to hear him tell Lee about it.

Lee choked up as he thanked Tom, and I loved my brother for his compassion. Soon Tom and I had to leave for Fort Rock, and Lee promised to see us there in a couple of weeks.

It was only June, but most of the land was already dry and parched. I wondered if the grass in the ditches had been green at all that spring. The few ranches that had drilled deep wells for irrigation stood out like emeralds on a brown quilt. Lizzy met us at the gate and rode the running board into the yard. Sunny was barking and wiggling so much I thought he'd have a stroke! I had missed him almost as much as the rest of the family. Ma was dusting flour off her hands when she stepped onto the porch, and I grabbed her in a bear hug while she screamed, "You'll get all messed up!" I was in heaven, finally being home.

My little sister, who was becoming a lovely young lady, had worked hard the months I was gone, helping Ma around the ranch. They decided to grow a few vegetables, which meant purchasing another barrel of water every week. Ma said growing their own vegetables didn't really save any money, but they enjoyed fresh vegetables so much. I sent Lizzy off to Aunt Fay's for a little vacation while I was home to help, and when she returned, we sent Ma away in spite of her protests. Feeling guilty about my easy life in Eugene, I scrubbed walls and floors, cleaned the stove, and helped Tom move the privy. Lizzy couldn't sit by and watch me work so we gave her the paint bucket and pointed to the gate and privy. Granny sent me home with some new curtains, and I had embroidered a new tablecloth over the winter. By the time Ma returned from Silver Lake, the house was ship-shape and she beamed at the changes.

Mona wrote that she found two part-time jobs, which she would have to give up when our hospital work began later in the summer. Granny's letters were full of news about her gardens and how much she enjoyed having Mona around the place.

One Sunday we packed a picnic lunch and Tom drove us to Sugar Pine Ridge where the pines produce enormous cones. Granny made beautiful Christmas wreaths with these which she sold in Eugene, so we always tried to make at least one trip to the ridge to collect baskets full. With our meal finished, Tom stretched out on a blanket in the cool shade of the pines, while Ma and I repacked dishes.

"Well Tom, I know you've been thinking hard about something… what is it?" Ma asked.

"How do you know I've got something on my mind?" Tom asked.

"You're my son, I just know. You've been as quiet as a church mouse lately. Ivy, do you know what's going on behind Tom's blue eyes?"

Tom answered for me; he sat up and faced Ma. "You've got it right. I've been waiting to find the right time to tell you something."

"Well?" Ma said, with an anxious look on her face.

"I've decided to join the Army," he said plainly. "I've already talked to a recruiter, and it's all but done. I want to work on airplanes, to learn a trade, and at the same time I'll be able to send you a steady allotment."

Tom and I watched for Ma's reaction.

Tom reassured her, "I know you're worried about what's going to happen to the ranch Ma, but we'll figure that out later. I love Fort Rock too, but I just have to try something else for awhile."

Ma sat up very straight, and then barely nodded.

"I do understand, Tom. If the Army is what you think is best, I trust your decision."

Ma became teary and we understood why. Her cousin was killed in World War I, so naturally she dreaded the thought of Tom serving in the Army if war broke out. Right then, France was trying to appease Germany, just to keep on their good side. It was an unspoken worry between us that the U.S. would enter the war if England were threatened. I've always felt it was best that we naively had no idea the world would spin out of control in just two years.

Lee was in Fort Rock only five days, and stayed with the family of his best high school friend. The moment I saw him get out of his truck, I knew he had big news. The expression on his face was relaxed, so like the Lee of better times. He wrapped an arm around my shoulders as we walked to the porch and pulled me aside.

"I want you to be the first to know that I've joined the Army, Ivy," he said, out of earshot of the others. "Mom was really upset, but I think she finally understands that I have to do something. Tom and I have talked a lot about it, and agree that we can't go wrong learning a trade and making money too."

I grasped Lee's hands and said, "Tom told Ma, and she took it better than expected. I'm very proud of you, Lee. I'm worried, but proud." We were so young. I can still see us standing there, just teenagers and playing at being adults.

"Will you write to me, Ivy?"

"Try and stop me!" I teased, and pulled him through the door where everyone waited.

The family embraced Lee's decision, just as they had Tom's. Each of our young men was to report in a matter of weeks: Tom to Portland, and Lee to Seattle. It was hard to imagine how much I would miss them. If I had known then how empty my heart would be when they left, and what the future held, I would have begged both of them not to join.

Lee missed ranch work; although he wouldn't drive past their old ranch that the bank owned, he showed up every afternoon to work around our place. I knew he spent mornings helping Terry, his school friend, on their ranch, but he said he had to keep busy or face the bare truth of his family's loss.

In the Oregon desert, amazing ice caves dot the landscape and have been used for thousands of years by the local tribes and pioneers. Some caves are large enough to explore, and offer a perfect place for families to gather to cool off. Generations of settlers visited these caves to fill buckets with blocks of ice to use at home. On the day before Lee left, Ma said if we'd get the ice from a cave about 4 miles away, she'd mix up ice cream for the evening. With the June temperature hitting 101 degrees, we welcomed the cool interior of the cave and weren't in a hurry to leave.

We talked about the Army, and Lee told me his recruiter suggested he try for one of the specialist schools. I had no doubt he would ace the tests, especially in math, and told him so.

"You're my biggest fan, Ivy. Mom and Dad aren't very supportive of this decision. The day I joined up, I felt twenty-five years old, standing in front of the recruiter. When I got home and told my folks, they acted like I was an irresponsible kid, deserting them. I wanted to yell that they were the ones who ruined their lives by living too high, but I kept quiet."

I told him, "Best that way. They know down deep that they have no one else to blame."

Lee used his pick ax to remove two buckets full of ice from the cave. Wrapped in old quilts and a tarp, hardly any melted before we got back home. With smaller tools we stabbed and gouged the blocks until the ice cream bucket was full of small chunks. Ma had the cream ready, and everyone took turns cranking until it was perfect. Tom found a music station on his radio, so we all danced up a storm, and forgot the troubles of the world.

By ten o'clock Ma was tired so I told her to go to bed and I'd clean up the kitchen. Lizzy disappeared with a book, and Tom winked as he said he'd leave us alone. Lee and I finished the dishes and he fastened the charm bracelet back onto my arm. He turned the charms over, admiring his choices.

"What charm would you like next?" he asked.

"Well, I think it should be a cow," I said, and he laughed heartily. "It would remind me of Brownie, and I do miss her when I'm away!"

I walked him to the truck, and suddenly Lee pulled me close, very close, and slowly, hesitantly, our lips met. I didn't know that I wanted to be kissed quite that way, but as soon as we touched I couldn't stop a little moan from escaping my throat. Then I remembered. I pulled away from Lee's grasp.

"Lee, I'm sorry, I...I can't."

"Why?" he asked. "All my life I've known we belong together. You know it too." His eyes searched mine and I knew I had hurt him. I loved Lee, but I was still unsure whether we'd have a life together.

I could only stammer, "There are things you don't know. Things I can't change." My heart was beating, no, hammering, in my chest, and suddenly I couldn't breathe.

Lee's arms wrapped protectively around my shoulders, and he led me to the corral bench.

"Ivy, there's nothing that could change my mind about how I feel."

I sobbed into his shoulder, "You just don't understand! Don't ask me to tell you!"

Lee pressed his lips against my temple, and quietly said, "I wish you'd trust me; we've been friends for so long, I thought we shared everything."

Tears streamed down my face as I said, "I'm so sorry."

Lee shook his head and I knew he was confused. I took his handkerchief to wipe my tears away.

"Promise me something, Ivy. I need you to say that you'll tell me your secrets someday…someday soon."

"I promise!" And I laughed a little, not forced or fake. Could I really confide in him? Not then, but I thought that perhaps when we were older he could forgive me.

I reached up to touch a lock of hair that fell across his forehead, and thought somewhat with wonder, how handsome that young man was, with his sandy hair and blue eyes. I trusted him with my very soul, but couldn't tell him yet.

# CHAPTER 8

AFTER LEE LEFT TO SPEND TIME WITH his family, I had just two more weeks at home with mine. My best friend, Edith, had a job in Silver Lake for the summer, but she came home every weekend. She was dating a young man from Paisley, who was a mechanic in the state's highway equipment garage. I'd never seen her so happy, and she said the same about me.

The news came that Fort Rock School would not reopen in the fall, and students would have to attend school in Silver Lake or board in Bend. The county wouldn't furnish a school bus to pick up the few students in Fort Rock, so for awhile it seemed that Lizzy would have to stay with Fay through the week. Just before school started, one of Fort Rock's laid off teachers was hired in Silver Lake, and for twenty-five cents a week from each student he could carry 5 students on his commute to and from school. I tried to convince Ma to move to Eugene, but she wouldn't hear of it. As if to encourage Ma's determination to stay on the ranch, southern Oregon received two good soaking rains over one week. Immediately the hills were covered with green carpets of tiny grass stems. The air smelled so fresh; we could overlook the muddy roads because at least the dust was settled.

Lizzy had grown like a weed over the year, so we spent my final two weeks home sewing blouses and skirts for her. She had become a beautiful teenager, and I was so proud of her sweetness. I might have been able to convince Lizzy to come live with me and Granny, but it wouldn't have been fair to Ma. After Tom and I left, Lizzy was all she had. When I returned to Eugene, Lizzy wrote often about school and new friends in Silver Lake. Some evenings, when I was too tired to eat after a day in the hospital, a letter from Lizzy would re-energize me.

Tom was working long shifts for the logging company before reporting to the base in Portland, and he decided to buy me a ticket on Bend-Eugene Stage Line, which ran a bus over the McKenzie Pass three days a week. Ma and Lizzy delivered me to the Bend Hotel early one morning, where I met the bus. I dreaded leaving them behind, but in the back of my mind, I was thinking about seeing Lee before he reported to boot camp in Seattle. He wrote saying he'd be at Granny's a few days after I arrived.

I was so happy to be back in Eugene that I wasn't nearly as home-sick as usual. Working in the gardens with Granny Ellen and Amy was soothing, with our female banter and their hilarious opinions on all subjects. Mona was busy working until our hospital shifts began, but we'd usually spend at least an hour before bedtime chatting about everything from guys to school.

At the hospital we were first assigned to change bed sheets, clean bedpans, bathe patients, and anything else the R.N.'s told us to do. Our shifts were ten hours long which included two hours of classroom instruction about sterile techniques and the prevention of hospital infections. During the final two weeks in the hospital we each shadowed an R.N., watching her clean wounds and apply dressings. The hospital work was demanding and almost frightening with the responsibility, but Mona and I both loved it.

On a Saturday morning I paced Granny's front porch, waiting for Lee to arrive to spend his last weekend with me before reporting to his base in Seattle. When I saw Lee bound from his pickup it seemed like months since we'd talked. After he had exchanged greetings with Granny and Mona, we slipped into the orchard, and Lee told me more about his family's money problems. His father's denial of their reduced situation had become a wedge in his parents' marriage, and they remained separated. There was nothing Lee could do about that part of the problem.

That afternoon Lee and Uncle Bob cut down several diseased old apple trees. The limbs were cut into wood stove length so Mona and I hauled the pieces to a stack by the old playhouse. It felt good to work alongside Lee, with his quiet take-charge assuredness. I felt so carefree and happy that I almost forgot what was hanging over my head.

Granny told us she heard on the radio that a dance was being held that night at the high school gym; everyone was invited. Mona declined an invitation to go with us, but Lee and I put on our best clothes and joined the crowd. It was a wonderfully lighthearted evening that extended into late-night coffee and donuts at a truck stop. I chattered on about nursing school, and Lee was equally excited about what the next few months held for him. When we kissed on Granny's front porch at two in the morning, I didn't pull away and came very close to confessing what ate at my soul. But I was afraid to risk seeing the hurt in his eyes. I wished so hard that I could forget that night with Paul. How could I expect Lee to forgive me when I couldn't forgive myself?

Watching Lee drive away the next morning sent me back to bed until Mona rousted me to help with Granny's pear harvest. The next week Lee and I began a correspondence that ran like clockwork for two years. During that time I saw him only twice, but we remained close in minds and hearts.

When our fall term began, Mona and I realized with a jolt that last year's classes were just a sample of what we faced. We had a full year of Anatomy and Physiology, plus Contagious Diseases, and Pharmacology. Again we were assigned to work in various departments at the hospital, but only two afternoons a week.

Ma wrote that Granny Ellen shouldn't worry about bringing canned fruits and vegetables to the ranch that fall, since she and Lizzy couldn't eat what was already in the cellar. Uncle Bob said he'd hunt for the winter's meat near Eugene instead of Fort Rock, and make sure Ma and Lizzy got some. After being unemployed for two years, Bob had just been hired by the Department of Forestry to maintain roads west of Eugene. I couldn't help but wonder at the rapid change in all our lives; old habits and routines had to adapt to new events.

As Thanksgiving approached, I talked Mona into going to Aunt Matilda's with Fay and me. Not only could we study together in the evenings, I thought she needed a little vacation. Mona soaked up the city, vowing that she would live in Portland some day. Fay treated us to a performance of *Girl Crazy* at the Hollywood Theater, straight from Broadway. The evening was magical, and I only wished Ma and Lizzy could've been there.

The letters from home were filled with encouraging news about increasing moisture in Fort Rock Valley. It wasn't enough to fill the tanks or ponds, but it looked promising for grass and hay. Even if it didn't last, the rain gave my family, and our neighbors, hope. I heard from Tom only occasionally; however he was good about writing Ma every week. After basic training, Tom was sent to Randolph Field near San Antonio, Texas, for Army Air Corps support training, and realized his dream of being an airplane mechanic. He faithfully sent most of his pay to Ma, and beyond using some to pay the taxes, I learned that she saved the rest for him. The café in Fort Rock where I had worked asked Ma if she'd cook breakfasts for them. She was so proud; for the first time in her life Ma was making a wage working for someone else. It was enough to take care of the few expenses that she and Lizzy had.

After Lee finished basic, he easily qualified for some engineering classes and was sent to Fort Lewis near Tacoma, Washington. No matter how overwhelmed I was with school and hospital work, I wrote Lee twice a week. Sometimes it was just a few lines; other nights I wrote pages about Granny and Mona, news from Ma and Lizzy about the ranch and Tom, and happenings at school and nurses training. He wrote that engineering classes were not too difficult for him, as long as he kept up with each day's instruction. After two months of schooling, twenty-five percent of his class was sent back to basic infantry or artillery training. I was so proud of Lee, and told him so!

Right after Thanksgiving Lee received orders transferring him to a larger engineering school in Georgia, and when he told me I barely kept from sobbing over the phone. The good news was that he would have two weeks leave during Christmas just before he left Fort Lewis. He planned to see his folks who had reunited in Portland, and then he asked if we could meet after my holiday visit in Fort Rock.

Lee boldly mentioned an idea, "Ivy, I've heard that a small town on the coast, Seaside, is a nice place to visit. There are several hotels there, and I thought that would be perfect for a quiet get-away. Of course, I would reserve two rooms."

I didn't hesitate a second, before saying, "Oh, yes!" So we planned that he would meet my bus in Portland on December 29th, and then we'd drive to the coast.

First I headed home; the snow was deep over McKenzie pass so the bus followed a highway department plow clearing the way. The bus was late getting into Bend, but Ma and Lizzy were waiting and I gathered them into my arms. They'd anticipated bad weather and drove over from Fort Rock a day earlier and were staying with Ma's cousin. We waited until the next morning for our trip home. She let me drive the old pickup for a change, which was very different from Uncle Bob's car that I used for Granny's errands. It was freezing in the pickup even with the heater going full blast; a rusty hole in the floor was covered with a piece of rug, but the frigid air still managed to surround our feet. I told Ma that one day we would be able to buy a new pickup for her, and she just waved off the suggestion.

Ma was beside herself, having both of her girls under her roof again. She was home from her job at the café by ten o'clock, so we had plenty of time to cook, play board games, sew, and gossip. The Grange had its usual Christmas dance, which I attended because Lizzy begged me to go. Just as I thought, it wasn't the same without Lee. All the neighbors and friends asked about my nursing school and about Lee, but they already knew where Tom was stationed. I told no one that I would see Lee very soon. Telling Ma the details was something I avoided, but she needed to know why I was leaving before New Year's Day. I couldn't lie to her, not after all we'd been through.

Lizzy was maturing into quite the young lady. Goodness flowed from her heart, and in many ways she reminded me of Mona. The mayor of Silver Lake planned a New Year's Eve dance in the state highway equipment barn, so we spent a night with Aunt Fay and shopped for fabric to make Lizzy a new dress.

The valley had more snowfall by Christmas than any winter in the last decade, so farmers and ranchers around Fort Rock and Silver Lake held their breaths that there might be a reversal beginning in the weather. One morning as I took the bucket from the kitchen to milk Brownie, Ma followed along to feed her chickens. The cold air bit my lungs so I pulled up the wool coat collar to cover my mouth and nose. We talked about Brownie, and that she should be freshened soon. Ma looked forward to getting a calf to sell, and improving Brownies milk production. Ma said I needed to buy some new shoes, and she could get them with her new wages. I knew how proud she was of those earnings and the ability to buy something I needed, so I didn't argue about taking the money.

"Ma, when I'm away I worry how you are getting along without Tom or me to help."

She shook her head and said, "We git along fine, and I actually enjoy workin' at the café. There's plenty of time for chores when I git home."

"One day we'll make it easier to live on the ranch." I crushed her to me, and kissed her smooth cheek. It was in my plan after college to work, and with Tom's help, we'd make enough money to have a deep well dug to irrigate fields of hay and rye. With water and feed, the ranch could support cattle again.

After milking was finished, I carried the bucket inside and sat down at the table while Ma filled two mugs with coffee. I had forgotten how good Brownie's cream tasted in Ma's coffee. We sipped in silence for a few minutes.

"I guess you're wondering why I'm leaving before New Year's. Lee has asked me to join him at a place on the coast before he leaves for Georgia." I waited for her response, and waited. At this point I hadn't looked straight at Ma, but finally I raised my eyes and met hers. She sat up very straight, as if to impart some sage advice or disapproval, but instead nodded and smiled, much as she had responded to Tom's enlistment announcement.

"You're a grown woman, Ivy, and smarter than most. I don't have to tell you what you can and can't do. I know what you're feelin', and I can't fault you for it. Lee will always think of you first and I think you'll do the same for him. Now, you go spend time with your fella, and don't worry about the rest of us."

Until that moment I hadn't admitted to myself how worried I was about Ma's reaction to my plan to go away with Lee, and found that I'd been holding my breath.

"Oh, Ma," I cried, "Thank you for understanding! I promise everything will be proper."

She cupped my face in her hands and said, "Anyone with half a brain can see how much you two care for each other."

I admitted to her that I hadn't found the strength to tell Lee everything about Paul.

"I have to tell him before he puts me on too high of a pedestal. It's not fair to him. Maybe he'll accuse me later of stringing him along. Oh, Ma, I'm so confused."

Ma just said, "Think very carefully before you do anything, Ivy. I understand what you are saying, but don't rush this decision." As usual, I felt better after Ma's advice.

When it was time to leave Fort Rock, Ma and Lizzy drove me back to Bend where I caught a different bus that took me straight to Portland. Guilt nagged at me for leaving early, but thoughts of seeing Lee again made me feel giddy!

When the bus pulled into the terminal in Portland, Lee was waiting. I absolutely melted into his arms, oblivious to anyone looking on. Our world existed only within the three feet wide bubble surrounding our embrace. Lee's uniform gave him the appearance of a more mature man, with worldly experience and self confidence, and I was proud to take his arm. Instead of driving the new highway to Seaside, Lee drove us to the train depot where we boarded for our trip to the coast. He decided we would enjoy lounging and visiting in our comfortable seats instead of driving the narrow, winding road in his spartan pickup. It was raining hard when the train pulled into the depot; the hotel had a car waiting for us, and soon we were settled in our respective rooms. I changed into a fresh dress, and we had supper in the hotel dining room. Afterward, when we sat in front of the lobby fireplace, fatigue caught up with me. Lee sweetly suggested we turn in, and he escorted me to my room.

Over the next four days we walked the stormy beach, shopped for souvenirs, and sampled seafood I had only dreamed about. Eating Dungeness crab was an art I attempted to master, but Lee cracked the shell so I could pick out the sweet, white meat. During the evenings we visited with other hotel guests, until they drifted upstairs. Once we were left alone in the late hour, we gazed at the fireplace embers, and talked quietly about what the next two years would bring. Lee wanted to be an engineer, building bridges and roads, and I dreamed of a career in a hospital. Oh, it seemed so simple, and we had no reason to think that our lives would follow any other path.

On the morning of the 31st, I answered a knock on my door and there stood Lee, with a single rose in his hand.

"Will you accompany me to celebrate New Year's Eve tonight, Miss Reese?" he asked with a bow.

I curtsied, and replied, "I'd be honored, Mr. Johnson." We laughed at each others' formality, and decided to have breakfast in a waterfront café. When we entered and I smelled the aroma of cinnamon from their famous rolls, it made me so homesick. By the time we slid into a booth overlooking the beach, tears spilled onto my cheeks. I told Lee that all of a sudden I missed Ma and Lizzy so much.

"I should have gone to the ranch instead of bringing you way out here," Lee said.

I wiped away my tears with his handkerchief, one that I had monogrammed with the Rocking J brand, and said "Oh, Lee, I'll be alright in a minute. It just caught me unprepared. I'm having a wonderful time here." For the rest of our morning we talked about our old school which had closed, and where some of our classmates were right then. Lee's best friend, Terry, was going into the U.S. Navy, and Edith was engaged to be married.

By early afternoon, the rain stopped so Lee suggested we go beachcombing. Salty spray hung in the air along the beach, and fog obliterated everything beyond fifty feet; it seemed we were alone on a deserted island. Regular scolding from the gulls that swooped over our heads made us laugh at their absurd squawking. Only an occasional bleat from foghorns reminded me we were not far from civilization. We took our scavenged treasures back to my hotel room, washed the sand away, and examined each one. Colored glass, smoothed by the combination of waves and sand, made up most of the collection.

We dressed up for the festivities, ate, danced, and joined a conga line that led us outside, around lampposts and returned through the back door. I sampled champagne for the first time and wondered what the big fuss was about it. Finally, the countdown to midnight began and we yelled "Happy New Year!" with the other revelers. We kissed with a sweetness that made me breathless. He was awakening sensations in me that I had suppressed for so long. Lee was the man I wanted, but I knew that a love based on deceit would grind a hole in our life together.

Lee's blue eyes softly looked into my heart, and he said, "Ivy, I do love you so much!" And I felt that love. We listened to sentimental music on the radio, broadcast from a ball room in New York City in the early hours of 1939.

A month later I received in the mail a new charm for my bracelet, a silver prong holding a small chunk of green glass, gleaned from the Seaside beach.

# CHAPTER 9

THE FIRST TIME I SAW A PATIENT die in the hospital I was stricken with guilt, as if I could have somehow prevented the outcome. I didn't know what to say to the family, and slipped out of the room in tears. Our nursing supervisor, Lenore Baker, took me into her office, and over a cup of tea she kindly impressed that I had to be strong and professional for the families. She assured me that everything possible had been done, and I was in no way responsible. She also said my reaction was common among new nursing students, which was a great relief. I was embarrassed at my actions, but the family asked her to let me know they appreciated the care I gave their mother at the end. Nurse Baker decided to incorporate a study unit on the topic for the whole class, and I discovered most of the students had the same insecurities. It was an early lesson in my career, and I tried to never again think about myself at a patient's bedside.

Study, work, eat, and sleep... in that order, filled the next two years for me and Mona. I saw Lee for two days in Portland during Thanksgiving holidays my junior year, when he finished with a two-week course in Portland. It was frustrating for us both, since so many other people demanded his attention. We had no time alone except the last night before he returned to Georgia. In the living room of his parents' apartment Lee clipped a new silver charm on my bracelet which joined the other five I had so far. I knew he pondered long and hard when it came time to choose one, and his thoughtfulness was endearing.

"I hoped you'd like this charm of a dancing couple, to remind you of the grange dances we used to attend at home," Lee said.

"It's wonderful Lee, and it does make me think of how we loved to dance back then, and again on our trip to Seaside," and we shared a laugh and a memory.

"I'm lucky to get your letters, Ivy. Some guys only get letters once a month or so. When I got your photo, there was a lot of whistling and teasing when I taped it inside my locker."

"You're my best friend, Lee. I'll never let you down," I said.

"You know we're more than friends, Ivy. It's time that you tell me what's been holding you back. This secret you have doesn't belong between us."

Every time I thought of Lee I was reminded of that secret, and I was beginning to worry I had made it worse by waiting so long to tell him. But still I could not say the words and watch his love turn to hate.

"Lee, I love you, surely you know that," I emotionally told him. It was the first time I'd come out and said the words. He sighed, smiled, and said he had waited a long time to hear it. We kissed passionately, but were aware that we were not alone in the apartment. I had borrowed Uncle Bob's car for the drive up to Portland, so we stole down the stairs and took it to a park by the river. We talked and kissed; when it was time to go back, he once again asked about my secret.

"Please, Ivy darling, let's put this behind us."

"The next time we meet, I will." As soon as I said that, he held me so close that I could hear his heart beating as fast as mine. I thought how I adored Lee, and would kill myself rather than hurt him. But there were bigger threats than just our little lives.

I told him that I wished he was not in the Army with all that was happening in Europe. Tom told Ma after Germany invaded Poland in September he didn't see how the U.S. could stay out of a war. In fact, he said we should step up and help fight Hitler.

Lee became very serious, and I was so proud when he said, "Even if I could end my enlistment, I wouldn't now. When I've finished engineering school, the Army will need us more than ever. The U.S. is beefing up all branches of our military, so when we enter the war, we'll be ready."

Germany wasn't the only aggressor I knew about. Japan continued to march through the Far East, obliterating whole villages in China and Southeast Asia. The Japanese seemed so foreign and far away, I couldn't see how they would be a threat to the U.S. I couldn't understand the concept of one country thinking they had the right to invade another for no reason other than greed.

Lee steered the conversation to Fort Rock, and I excitedly told him that Ma was sure she'd be able to run cattle on the range soon. Even though his family lost their ranch, Lee was genuinely excited about our tentative good fortune. We sadly parted the next day, and I had to remind myself that I'd even seen Lee; our time together was so brief.

A month later I convinced Mona to go home with me for a week. She won a small scholarship that year, so the pressure of working so much had been lifted. Ma and Lizzy had listened to me talk about Mona so often they felt they already knew her, and vice-versa. Christmas was quite merry at the ranch. Ma hadn't told me that the well was once again producing water for the house; Lizzy slyly showed Mona the bathroom, then giggled at the look of surprise on my face. A flushing toilet turned a shabby ranch house into a quaint country home.

When England and Canada declared war on Germany, I was

certain the U.S. would do the same; then Germany invaded France in May of 1940. Tom expected to be shipped to Europe; however politics played another hand. We waited and watched.

The summer before my senior year of nursing school I had to train full time at the hospital. Most of the time Mona and I had the same shift, and we worked a lot of nights together. Granny Ellen worried that we weren't getting enough rest when on our days off sometimes we'd go dancing at a pavilion by the river. Mona met a young man there, who was the bookkeeper for a logging company west of Eugene. He was very serious about Mona, and I thought maybe they'd get engaged. She was level-headed though, and said nothing was going to get in her way of finishing school. I enjoyed dancing with all the young men, but ended up comparing them to Lee. No one could measure up to my darling.

In June, the hospital faced a crush of measles cases which had morphed into severe complications that sometimes weren't treatable at home. It was heartbreaking to see children suffering from high fevers that occasionally led to ear infections or even deafness. Some had their sight affected, and in two cases the children died of meningitis. Because the disease was so contagious, most parents avoided taking their families to public places; parks were eerily empty a few weeks in early summer. Once the measles had run its course, another epidemic tried to take hold in the city. Polio was raging in Portland, with hospitals and parents frantically fighting the spread of the most dreaded disease of that time. Eugene adopted quarantine measures which were fought by some residents as "too restrictive;" however, the effort was rewarded with a far less number of cases than neighboring cities. Most of that summer was lost in a haze of long hours at the hospital, and a hope of peace in Europe.

Soon it was evident that peace was still out of reach when, in July of 1940, Germany launched a massive aerial bombardment on England, targeting ships in the Channel and airfields along the coast. By September, English towns and factories were in the sights of Hitler's pilots, with the devastating result being hundreds of civilians killed. Whole neighborhoods were pounded into rubble each night, but still England held on. And the U.S. continued to wait.

After the polio quarantine was lifted, Ma and Lizzy took the bus to Eugene for a visit, when our neighbor offered to take care of the barnyard animals. It was a wonderful time for all of us, especially for Granny. The first time I wore my student-nurse dress and cap, Ma beamed and Lizzy exclaimed that I looked very professional. Their compliments meant more to me than anything anyone else could say. Ma had sacrificed so much for us; she deserved a good life and I planned to make it happen. Actually, Ma looked younger and healthier than I remembered. During one of our evening family chats on the porch, Granny declared that Lizzy should plan on going to college at the university and live with her as I had. From that moment, I believe Lizzy started planning her college life.

Tom was home on leave that fall, and told us that he was being shipped to California for specialized training. He was still anxious for the country to enter the war. Lee wrote that some fellows he knew from his year in college had joined the Canadian Air Force to fight the Germans. If he hadn't already been in the Army, I believe Lee would've been one of those fellows joining up in Canada.

Our nursing class had a number of students drop out by our senior year, due to financial problems, marriage, or grades. After working in the hospitals directly with patients, some students decided they weren't suited to the nursing career. For me, helping people get well or making them comfortable, was all I ever wanted. Nurse Baker's guidance for working with the families of terribly ill or dying patients prepared us all for what lay ahead.

During my Thanksgiving visit with Aunt Matilda, she was so impressed with my success in nursing school she decided to give me a monthly stipend in addition to paying my tuition. I was in desperate need of clothes and good shoes, and relieved that Ma could spend her earnings on Lizzy instead of me. My great aunt was very frail that fall, so her nieces advised her to hire a companion who spent all day in her home until one of them came to stay the night. I wrote Aunt Matilda often, knowing how she loved to receive letters. I could never repay the kindness she showed when helping me realize my dreams. She only asked that I, in turn, help someone else.

Mona and I became workaholics, either studying or working at the hospital every day. We'd been discussing where we'd go after graduation, since neither of us planned to return home permanently. Mona was the most skilled nurse in our class, and she considered studying operating room techniques after she worked a year or so. Poring over medical magazines that advertised nursing jobs, one day we'd plan to apply at a hospital in Los Angeles; the next week Seattle was on top of our list.

Looming over my head, like an anvil ready to drop, was my heartbreaking secret. I finally told the whole story to Mona, knowing that she would never judge my mistakes. She clucked at me like a mother hen, and said I was making too much of the issue. Mona advised me to keep the secret to myself, and make a life with Lee. If I felt like I had to tell him, I should do it right away, before any more time elapsed. I practiced just how the conversation would go, however there wasn't a version of the scenario where Lee's eyes didn't register confusion and pain at my betrayal. I cried all through that night and was such a mess the next morning that I had Mona report that I was sick. Granny checked on me a few times, but I stayed in bed, rolled up tight in my quilt. In the end I was glad Lee was so far away so I didn't have to meet him face to face.

For the next two weeks I jumped back and forth, practicing each scenario in my head, first to keep the secret, then to tell Lee everything. To my thinking, keeping this from him was running a risk, because there was always a chance he might find out. That would be worse than my telling him right away. My heart broke every time I played the scene to the end, and my body shook as if Lee was present, hearing my story. Would I want to know if Lee had made love to some other girl? My answer was "no;" however, that was like comparing apples to oranges. Girls were held to a higher standard, and we were weaned in that custom.

Nestled into bed one evening when I was home for the Christmas holidays, I composed the letter I should have written several years earlier. Sobbing over the pale blue stationary that Edith gave me so long ago, I felt that what I had to confess would kill any love he had for me, but I held out hope it wasn't so. My hand shook so much as I wrote, I had to copy it over three times.

*Dearest Lee,*

*I've dreaded telling you something that has gripped my heart with cold hands for these last several years. You've asked me to tell you what holds me back, and this is the only way I can bear to reveal the dark secret that looms over our future.*

*You were right in assuming that Paul had something to do with my mood after he left. I was fooled into thinking he loved me, and we became intimate one evening. I was so ashamed afterwards, but it was my fault this happened. Soon we all knew he had deceived everyone.*

*I've had such guilt all these years, and can't bear to think of the pain you have right now. You must feel terribly betrayed, and I realize this most likely will ruin any chance we have of a future together.*

*My only hope is that you can forgive me, but if that's not the case, I understand. I've not been able to forgive myself.*

*Please stay out of danger in this troubled world.*

*With all my love, Ivy*

As soon as the letter was posted, I second guessed what I'd done and it put me in a depressed mood for the rest of the holidays. Although I convinced myself that I wouldn't get a response, I still checked the mail every day and was devastated when I didn't hear from Lee professing his forgiveness. About a month later Tom wrote that Lee had been shipped to the South Pacific. Lee never wrote me back.

# CHAPTER 10

SCHOOL WAS MY SALVATION, AND I ATTACKED the last term, according to Granny, "like a cat with my tail on fire!" The spring months were spent in the hospital, mostly in the emergency room. I saw firsthand devastating car crash injuries, gunshot victims, terrible burns, and bacterial infections. One young doctor asked me to help him deliver a baby just as the mother arrived at the hospital entrance. Everything happened so fast; if I already didn't know what to do, it was too late if I had to ask someone. The pressure was staggering, but I had no idea I would use the methods learned in the ER early in my nursing career.

A group of about ten nursing students decided one Saturday night to see the new movie, *The Wizard of Oz*, starring Judy Garland. We'd never seen anything like it before, and Mona would break into "Somewhere over the Rainbow" anytime she felt we needed a boost! Her positive attitude raised my spirits time and time again over the next few years, when I needed it the most.

When we were within a month of completing our degrees, Mona and I seriously discussed what each of us had been mulling over: where to take our knowledge. Several hospitals in the area were eager to hire graduates; even the big institutions in Portland sent letters to all the nurses bragging on the benefits coming our way if we'd sign on with them. We thought alike, Mona and I. She astounded me repeatedly, when a comment would jump from her mouth, just as I formed it in my mind. Being six years older, her maturity was evident; however, she never made me feel as if she could pull rank because of it. We wanted to leave the university together, and work side by side as we'd always done.

Graduation day arrived in May of 1941, and Mona's mother surprised her by coming to see her daughter receive the diploma. They had corresponded very little over the four years, and I never expected to meet Mrs. McWhirter. I felt like a million dollars when I walked across the stage and shook hands with the university president. In a way, it seemed to have taken ten years to get my degree; other times the years were only a blip in my memory. Granny Ellen's house was brimming with guests since she insisted that everyone stay in the usually empty rooms of the old boarding house. With Uncle Bob's new income, some repairs were completed in the empty rooms upstairs. Once Mona and I dusted and aired the old rooms, washed linens and windows, and scrubbed ancient bathrooms, we were ready for company. It was worth all the work when everyone gathered after the graduation ceremony for the party. Mrs. McWhirter and Ma visited like two old friends, each bragging about the other's daughter. Uncle Bob and Amy roasted a pig on a spit in the orchard, and announced to the neighbors that they were invited.

Mona and I looked snappy in our nursing capes, caps, and pins and we were swarmed by several neighborhood girls, asking questions and wondering whether they too could achieve their dreams. I hardly believed my luck of having graduated from college. Great-aunt Matilda could not make the trip to Eugene, but I called her right after the ceremony assuring that I would visit her soon and tell her all about the big day. As the crowd dispersed, and guests drifted off to bed about midnight, Ma and I sat in the parlor having a cup of hot tea.

Ma reached over and patted my knee, asking, "Well, now that you have that degree, Ivy, what will you do with it? I'm sure you have some kind of plan. Another thing I want to know is why didn't you tell me you and Lee broke up?"

"Ma, I wrote Lee at Christmas and told him everything about Paul...everything," I answered, with a catch in my throat and my chin held at a determined angle.

"Oh! What did he say?" she asked, taking my hands.

"Not a thing. Not a darn thing. I haven't heard a word from him since then," I said, with tears streaming down my cheeks. "So I was right that he couldn't bear knowing, and I couldn't bear keeping the secret to myself."

Ma leaned over to look squarely at me, and said, "Lee will think it over and come 'round in time."

"I wish I believed you!" I sobbed into her shoulder for all the unhappiness I had caused.

Lizzy came stumbling downstairs at that moment and asked what I was crying about. Ma and I quickly straightened up and wiped our faces.

"If you must know, it's because I am going to miss you so much! Ma, I was just going to tell you that Mona and I have joined the Army Nurse Corps. We will report as soon as she returns from Idaho next month!" I confessed, watching in amusement as their mouths dropped open in surprise. I was the first to explore the idea of military nursing, after a patient told me about her sister going overseas as a Navy nurse. Mona immediately seized on the idea, which led to a visit with a recruiter.

"Are you sure it's what you want to do?" Ma asked, shakily.

"I'm not really sure about anything, but in the meantime I'll get to travel, use my nursing degree, and send money home! We've heard from several sources that Army hospitals offer opportunities for training in new specialties, and the pay is good."

Lizzy laughed that I was crazy, but added that she was so jealous! Ma put her face in her hands, laughing and crying at the same time.

"You are an unpredictable girl, Ivy! But promise me, after you have seen the world, come back to Fort Rock."

Although I had no plans to move back to Fort Rock, at that moment I told her I would.

I said to her, "I want you to arrange to have a deep well dug on the ranch; Tom and I've discussed it, and he checked with the bank in Bend. They will loan us the money for the well, and you can use our allotments to make the payments. See, we have it all figured out!"

Ma then smiled slyly, and said, "You won't have to borrow too much from the bank for the well. I've been saving Tom's allotment, and it'll pay for more than half the cost if he wants to use it that way. I wrote Aunt Matilda that I could pay your tuition last year, but the sweet dear insisted she'd rather take care of it."

We spent the evening planning ranch improvements, and I pushed Lee out of my mind. The next day we left to see Aunt Matilda in Portland; before the week ended, we were home in the valley.

The desert around Fort Rock bloomed with renewed gusto that spring, reminiscent of my early childhood memories. Lizzy and I often hiked up some of the area buttes, and explored ice caves around the buttes' bases. One morning while Ma was cooking at the café, we strolled across the pasture to fetch Brownie, admiring all the different wildflowers that shared our part of the valley. Striding through the blossoms, we caught their fragrances rising in our wake, releasing a heady perfume unmatched by a bottle's contents. Suddenly, thousands of butterflies rose in a confetti-like mass, swirling and dipping like a cape in the wind. It was breathlessly beautiful, and later Lizzy and I tried to describe the scene.

"Oh, Ma, you should have seen it!" Lizzy breathlessly reported.

"What kind of butterflies were they?" she asked.

"I don't know, just pretty ones," I said. "Why?"

"Butterflies come from caterpillars, and I just wondered what they had been chewing on in my field," Ma pointedly said.

"Who cares?" Lizzy retorted. "It's worth it, just to see the butterflies!"

"I guess I'm too worried about plague and famine, after all the years of drought. I remember as a young bride when a cloud of grasshoppers ate everything in the fields and the clothes drying on the line," Ma shared. "It was a terrible time."

"I think things are looking up," I told her, "so I don't want you to worry anymore! The Reese Ranch is on its way to producing hay and beef once again! As soon as the deep well is pumping, we should hire a farm hand to help plant and irrigate the fields, and after that you can start buying cattle."

Tears welled up in Ma's eyes, and she admitted that having cattle on the land again seemed farfetched just a few years earlier. So much had changed since that summer of 1937. The pride I felt of having a career ahead gave me purpose and I felt good about making it possible to improve the ranch. Ma wanted it to be as viable as in the past, and she deserved it. Tom and I would also see to it that Lizzy could attend college if she so wished.

Before I left Fort Rock, Edith drove up from Paisley to show off her new wedding band. My old friend had exactly the life she dreamed about, and was confused that I had broken up with Lee, since I'd never shared with her the secret about Paul.

"You'll get back together, I just know it. True love never quits," she declared, and I wanted to believe her. Edith was concerned that the war in Europe might drag the U.S. into the conflict, and take her new husband away. Her talk about their plans to save money and open their own mechanic's garage in Lakeview was infectious, and soon I was telling her about our plans for the ranch. Edith was absolutely glowing with happiness and I was envious of their simple love for each other.

The weeks I spent in Fort Rock were blissfully quiet, and I was tempted at times to write Lee's mother. In the end, I decided that wouldn't be fair to her. Tom and Lee kept up with each other, so I knew I'd find out if he were injured or worse. Against all hope, I kept thinking that Lee would drive up to the house in his old pickup, sweep me into his arms, and we'd live happily ever after. After all the months since I wrote to Lee, he remained foremost in my mind; however, I accepted that I had to let him go. His silence made it plain our connection was history. I did want someone in my life. An adventure lay at my feet, taking me into strange lands to meet new people, and I felt that, given time, it would help my heart heal.

On July 1st, 1941, Mona and I met in Bend and reported together to the Portland recruiting office. Regulations dictated that hair must be worn short, and I anxiously submitted to the shearing. Without the weight of my long braids which I usually wrapped in a bun, the short hair style curled softly around my face. That was our first step towards becoming members of the military Two weeks later we arrived by train at Fort Sam Houston in San Antonio, Texas. The first thing we noticed was how humid South Texas was, in addition to the heat. We showered morning and evening, and still never felt fresh. We slept with the windows open to catch any breeze, which meant the mosquito netting that draped over our beds had to stay tightly tucked around the mattresses. Since army nurses were given a rank of Second Lieutenant, protocol dictated who we could date, or even spend time with. Some of the nurses had to learn the hard way, and soon kept their social contacts limited to officers. Our training was six weeks long, covering how the military practiced medicine.

The Army Nurse Corps ranks at Fort Sam Houston was broken into units of about eighty women. I was astounded at the range of diversity among the recruits, who hailed from California and Washington to Oklahoma and Louisiana. Some women had already worked years in hospitals, and others were just out of school like me.

One of the instructors, an attractive nurse in her thirties, had just returned from Manila in the Philippines. She echoed the opinion that the posting was "posh" with comfortable dorms and modern hospitals. American women were in short supply, so the nurses were in high demand at dances, dinners, and beach parties. I thought going overseas would be just what I needed to reinvent myself. The dances at Fort Sam Houston gave Mona and me an excuse to wear our dress uniforms and I felt proud as a peacock. It was the first time I truly felt carefree. At the termination of our brief training, we were given the choice of being stationed at a U.S. Army hospital in the states, or volunteering for overseas duty. Since we chose to go overseas, Mona and I were granted two-weeks leave.

My orders were to spend a year in the Philippine Islands, which was far too long according to Ma.

"Well, I guess you'll have Mona with you for company, so maybe you won't be too homesick," she said.

"And if you get sick over there, at least you'll know a doctor," Mother added, which caused Lizzy and me to moan.

The new well was drilled right after I left for San Francisco, our disembarkation point. Ma had already begun making improvements on the ranch. With running water in the house again, she added a hot water heater, fired with an oil burner. No more having to heat water on the stove top and carry the sloshing pan to the tub! Oh, how I wished for electricity and a phone for Ma; however it was another twelve or thirteen years before those modern conveniences arrived in Fort Rock Valley.

San Francisco was so much like a scene from the movies, with steep streets, beautiful old houses, and streetcars; I expected to see Myrna Loy or Cary Grant strolling along the sidewalks. Mona had never seen the ocean, so standing on the pier, looking across that blue expanse overwhelmed her for a few days. By the time we boarded the transport she was ready and willing! For me, the very smell of the sea brought to mind the time Lee and I stayed in Seaside.

As our ship slowly moved away from the docks, we stood at the rail, waving to strangers on the pier who waved back. I thought to myself, "Well, Ivy, here you go! My next stop is half-way around the world!"

# CHAPTER 11

LIFE ABOARD THE SHIP WAS GAY, CAREFREE, and quite romantic, using the word loosely. All of the women were at least twenty-one years old and male officers were usually older. In spite of commanding officers' admonishments about conduct becoming gentlemen and ladies, alcohol flowed freely which wiped out inhibitions. The Army Nurse Corps admitted only single women, but we were aware that many doctors and other officers had wives back in the states. The nurses were out for a good time, which led several to behave with abandon and look like hell the next morning. I loved to dance the night away and managed to find a couple of partners who made it plain they also wanted nothing to do with quick romances aboard the ship either. They'd share photos of families and get teary after too many beers, but I admired them for their faithfulness.

I had assumed that once on board we nurses would receive more instruction regarding our duties in the Philippines, but I was very wrong. We slept until nine each morning, ate breakfast, and then hand washed a few pieces of clothing. Mona and I played shuffleboard or cards until lunch. Every meal was marvelous, and we dressed for dinner every night. Mona and I were advised to pack several long dresses for the voyage and the social scene in Manila. At first Mona reveled in the night life, but towards the end of our voyage, she too retreated to our shared room for peace and quiet. The day before we made landing in Manila, I wrote long letters home to Ma, Tom and Granny Ellen describing everything so far.

On September 22, 1941 we were greeted at the Manila dock by a crowd of military members, civilians, and a military band. Most of our group was assigned to Sternberg Hospital in Manila, and other nurses were sent to various hospitals across the city or in rural areas. There were no drab nurses' quarters at Sternberg; in the colonial hotel we lounged on pastel cushions and were cooled by large ceiling fans. Our laundry was taken away each morning, and returned that evening pressed and folded perfectly. Meals were quite elegant, prepared by skilled cooks and served on delicate bone china. Every evening men and women officers gathered after dinner for dancing, cards and general pairing off. Our patient load was quite easy, with few emergencies, so all members of the staff had time for tennis, swimming, and even polo matches. Sometimes I felt like Dorothy in the land of Oz: I came from a gray life into a world of wondrous colors and adventure.

I was certain that Mona and I weren't the only nurses who felt out of place in that world of decadence and privilege. When I sat down to a five course meal of hearty servings, I could only think about Ma scratching together enough for her family during our hardest years on the ranch. She would have been appalled at the waste carried away from the officers' tables. I remember hoping that some of the food was salvaged for the Filipino kitchen workers. Wine and beer flowed endlessly, and sometimes I worried that the doctors were not just drinking after their shifts ended. In the beginning, some young nurses were afflicted with idol worship concerning the military doctors. After a few weeks of observing those doctors more concerned with their rendezvous each evening, than their patients, I became frustrated and said as much. Mona decided it had to do with being so far from home, away from restrictions of family life, in a tropical paradise. It was no excuse, and none of my business, but I chafed at the misconduct. Since it occurred from the top brass down to lesser ranking soldiers, no one was disciplined.

Transports came and went: very sick soldiers were shipped to the U.S. and replacements arrived regularly. General MacArthur was building up forces in the Philippines against a perceived threat from the Japanese. Knowing that, I still felt safe because we knew the general's wife and son were with him in Manila. I thought that surely he wouldn't have them with him if there was much danger. One very real immediate threat in the tropics was disease. Malaria and dengue fever were just two of many dangerous, miserable maladies. Quinine tablets were freely dispensed, and mosquito netting was draped over all beds. Still, even with such precautions, cases of malaria regularly put nurses, doctors, soldiers, and civilians in bed with chills and fevers.

One night, while Mona and I lounged in the rattan chairs on the screened-in porch off our bedroom, we talked about our first two months in Manila.

"I love what we are doing here," I said, "but are we just kidding ourselves about how safe we are? I got a letter from Ma today, and she says there are lots of rumors in the news about a massive Japanese force moving south. I don't know how her letter made it through the censors. She's really worried about us, and I want to write back that everything is going to be alright. But I don't know that."

"Do like I did," Mona said. "Lie! I told my mother we are very secure, and not to worry. Actually, I have to keep telling myself that to sleep at night. There's nothing we can do about the situation, so I'll just keep doing my job and let the generals do theirs."

I laughed at her pragmatism, and said, "Mona, my wise friend, you are right!"

Most of the nurses used the opportunity in Manila to shop for exotic and lovely clothes. Ma was getting a major portion of my allotment, so I wasn't as tempted as the others. Mona had a weakness for shoes, saying that she seldom had more than one pair at a time as a child. I did splurge on one item; I bought a tiny silver charm of a palm tree for the bracelet Lee gave me. When I wore it each evening at dinner, I thought of Fort Rock and home. The ring Ma gave me for high school graduation was left with her for safe-keeping, but I couldn't leave the bracelet.

Ma wrote that the new well was completed, with a generator to run the pump for irrigation. Her new farm hand was the son of a family in Silver Lake. Ma planned to get fields of alfalfa and rye planted and a few head of cattle bought in the spring. Ma wouldn't give up her morning cooking job at the café, saying she enjoyed the company of early risers. A letter from Lizzy arrived once a week, with news mostly of school and friends. She always told me what the ranch looked like, and how happy Ma was lately. Lizzy was dating a boy whose father was a lawyer in Lakeview. They couldn't go out alone, but Lizzy was allowed to date as long as another couple joined them. I thought how Lizzy had an advantage of a bigger world while growing up, and wished I hadn't been so naïve. In spite of that, I had made a good life; my only regret was not having Lee as part of it. Lizzy decided she wanted to be an English teacher, so talk of college was a common topic. We planned that by the time she needed money for college, the well would be paid off, and my allotment would pay her school expenses.

A letter from Tom said that he was being shipped to Baltimore, and from there would be in an undisclosed foreign country by Christmas, which vexed Ma more than ever. His training as a bomber mechanic was valued even before the war began, and we later learned that his overseas service began in Iceland in November of 1941. At that time I wondered if Lee was still somewhere in the South Pacific.

Mona was eager to shop for Christmas presents in the local businesses with her newly acquired income. We were told to have our packages ready by Thanksgiving, to arrive in the U.S. on time. I bought Ma a woven coverlet for her bed, in her favorite colors. For Lizzy I chose a string of pearls with matching earrings. Since we had no address for Tom yet, his gift would have to wait. I bought Mona a pair of red patent slippers that reminded me of those worn by Dorothy in the Land of Oz Many mornings she woke me up by singing the rainbow song loudly in the shower.

Around the first of December, I got a letter from Ma with sad and shocking news about my brother Michael. Sheriff Newberry came to the house with an official document that said Michael had been killed in an oil rig accident in Texas. A week after the sheriff's visit, Ma got a letter from a woman who said she was Michael's wife. They had a baby boy that she called Mike. She told my Ma that Michael had planned to come home for a visit, that he was a good husband and father. Ma sent her money to get a bus ticket for the two of them, and thought they'd be in Fort Rock before Christmas. I hoped Ma wasn't being tricked into sending money, but she sounded so happy, after having to bear such terrible news of Michael's death.

Lizzy wrote a short letter that I received on the sixth day of December, which contained another bombshell. She informed me that our own Ma was seeing a gentleman she met in the café. Ma hadn't said anything to me since I was so far away and she wasn't sure how I'd feel. Mr. Atkins owned a grocery store in Lakeview, and travelled through Fort Rock to Bend often to pick up goods. He was a widower with a grown son who lived near Seattle. Since Ma invited him to dinner at the ranch, Lizzy had the opportunity to meet him. Her opinion was that he seemed to be a good man and helped Ma after the news about Michael. Truthfully, I was delighted for Ma; she deserved all the happiness the world could give her. Lizzy seemed excited to meet Michael's widow and baby and I wondered if Tom knew all this. I planned to write Lizzy a letter after Christmas telling her that when she thought the time was right, she could tell our Ma that I was pleased to hear about her new beau. For the first time since arriving in Manila, I missed the ranch.

# CHAPTER 12

MABEL STARKY BURST INTO THE WARD SHOUTING, "Pearl Harbor has been bombed by the Japanese!" Screams of "No!" and "It can't be true!" fell from a hundred lips. In a matter of a few minutes, our whole building switched from polite voices and muffled conversations to chaos, no matter how hard staff tried to calm the patients. We could hear cries coming from the women's ward; even we nurses had panicked looks on our faces, which did nothing to help the situation. Suddenly, Chief Nurse Captain Roberts rounded up the on-duty staff, and sternly admonished us for letting our emotions and fear affect the patients.

"You will be calm and instill an air of control over their safety. Everyone, including me, is worried that the Philippine Islands are next, but we are Army and you are nurses!" she warned, in her clipped, staccato words.

We left the small office feeling ashamed, but resolved to serenely return to our nursing duties, presenting brave and confident faces.

Reports began trickling in about the devastation in Hawaii. Then the unthinkable happened the very same day: the Japanese attacked several airfields in the Philippines and hospitals in more remote locations. We kept our fingers crossed that Manila would be spared. Later that day the hospital at Fort Stotsenberg, seventy-five miles north of Manila, sent out a plea for help. Nearby Clark Field had been bombed, and hospital staff there needed reinforcements. Captain Roberts asked for volunteers. Mona and I stepped forward, but she ordered Mona to stay and assist in surgery when cases began arriving. I was temporarily assigned to remain at Sternberg in the burn ward. The five volunteers quickly packed changes of clothes and toiletries, and arrived back at the hospital just in time to climb in the back of a canvas covered truck. Those nurses were tasked with stabilizing the injured and evacuating them to Manila.

I can barely remember those first few days, with injured soldiers and civilians swelling the hospital wards. At one time, patients were placed on pallets spread across the lawn, until we gained use of a church and other nearby buildings. Japanese planes droned overhead day and night, on their way to targets. Finally, three days after the Pearl Harbor strike, the port of Manila was bombed. Day by day more buildings, businesses, schools, warehouses, and neighborhoods were reduced to rubble, and the injured kept streaming into Sternberg Hospital. General MacArthur announced that help was on the way, but he couldn't even estimate when troops would arrive. Lookouts scanned the vast ocean's horizon, hoping to see a convoy steaming to our rescue. In the meantime, troops in the Philippines were repositioned, batteries fortified, and a defensive strategy planned. Judging by the numbers of wounded soldiers taken in at the hospital, I wondered how we had anyone left in the field. When the Stotsenberg Hospital evacuees began swamping our wards, we realized that without relief, bandages and other supplies would soon be depleted.

The white dresses we wore during our shifts, the traditional nurses' uniform that set us apart from civilian volunteers, vexed us all since the skirts and sleeves were too long. For bedside nursing in traditional situations, we ladies in white invoked calmness and security in the wards. However, we found ourselves jumping across cots and pallets, moving patients by grabbing their arms and legs to pull them onto stretchers, and working in the open where mud was ankle deep. Nurse Roberts asked for, and was granted permission to adapt men's olive-drab coveralls for our nursing uniforms. Mona and I looked at each other dressed in the baggy clothes, and doubled up laughing. We needed something to laugh about in those days of blood, burnt skin, and screams of pain.

In a matter of days, the United States was at war on two fronts: President Roosevelt and congress declared war on Germany and Japan. The U.S. entered the war at last. I wondered about Ma, and what she knew about the bombings in Manila. I scribbled off a note, but as far as I knew, only official dispatches were leaving Manila.

Rumors raged throughout Manila that U.S. forces were nearing the Philippines and would soon demolish the Japanese, then transport us all back to safety. Every so often someone would report that smokestacks were on the horizon; however, hope dissolved into despair time after time.

I had little time to reflect on my personal life aside from physical needs. When I did think about home, Mother and Lizzy were immediately in my thoughts. I hated to think of how worried they must be. I wondered if Michael's young widow and baby were at the ranch yet. For many months I had steeled my heart against dreaming about Lee, and what could have been. Since the bombing of Manila, those dreams provided the escape I needed from the gore and suffering that surrounded me each and every day. I replayed all the times Lee and I danced together, touched and laughed, and even felt the catch in my throat when recalling how his arms felt around me. In hindsight, I would have given anything to not have told him about my involvement with Paul. After all that happened since I wrote the letter, it became clear that my secret wasn't all that important. In my naïveté I caused a lot of unhappiness.

Mona was my savior, bless her soul! Our hotel had been turned into women's wards, so we moved our belongings into a linen closet in the main hospital. We slept on thin straw-filled mattresses sewn together by a kind cook's helper. Each morning when we unfolded our arms and legs from cramped positions, Mona would exit the closet singing, "Some WHERE, O-verrrr the Rainbow, Waaay up High...," on her way to the bathroom, and anyone who was able, would join in with her. As the hospital filled with patients from the civilian population, we noticed that the rations were cut back a little each week. I knew the storerooms were filled with plenty of food, and thought that high ranking officials must have worried early in the war that we would be pinned down longer than they let on.

The Japanese continued bombing Manila, mangling bodies and destroying buildings, never considering whether the victims were soldiers or civilians. We nurses hurried from patient to patient, deciding who could be saved, and those who only needed dulling of their pain before death relieved them from their suffering. Mona spent hours on her feet in the operating room each day, but wouldn't ask to be relieved until she was close to collapsing. As long as the doctors were in surgery, they needed her there. In the states, Mona wouldn't have been allowed to assist in surgery, but her uncertified skills were appreciated in Manila. I spent half of my time in the burn unit, only because no one else would willingly take the duty except our supervisor, Captain Roberts. The hours I spent in the women's wards were pleasant in comparison. A number of civilian women came in with pregnancy problems and injuries, children were sick with dysentery, and every day or so a new baby joined the hospital's numbers. Added to these usual medical issues, we began receiving civilian casualties from the Japanese bombing runs.

MacArthur's troops were hurriedly building defensive measures to repel the Japanese if they made a landfall, but the aerial assaults kept a steady number of casualties streaming into the hospital. Young soldiers suffered horrible burns and injuries, and at that time our medicine chest was full of drugs and supplies to care for them. Since we were Army nurses, our unit was finally assigned to administer first to the soldiers, and Filipino nurses and aides took over the civilian wards. By December 20, patients once again overflowed the buildings, onto patios, lawns, and verandas where it was more difficult to keep the cots covered with mosquito netting. Quinine was dispensed freely as a preventative, and again during malarial attacks; however I knew that the supply wasn't bottomless.

The bombardment of Manila jangled everyone's nerves. The hospital took a few hits, causing several casualties. I felt helpless, trying to care for so many injured soldiers lying unprotected in the open, when we didn't know where the next shell would explode. Some days the rumbling and pounding would finally force me under a table as I tried to escape from the deafening noise. Often, when my shift ended and I returned to the building where we ate, I noticed that my hearing was no better than having cotton in my ears.

On one occasion I was sent to escort several nuns from a girls' school to assist in the civilian wards. It had been over two weeks since I had ventured away from the hospital. The destruction across Manila was shocking, and it became clear why the hospital was inundated with so many maimed residents and soldiers. I honestly couldn't understand how anyone survived the air attacks. The girls' school closed when the bombings began, and the nuns were terribly afraid to stay in their abandoned building. As we made our way back through the city, the whine of approaching enemy aircraft prompted our scramble for cover, but we all arrived at Sternberg with only scrapes and bruises.

After having those nuns at the hospital for a week, we all agreed with Captain Roberts that they were worth their weight in gold.

On December 22 we learned that over forty thousand Japanese troops landed onshore south of Manila. General MacArthur moved his operations and family to Bataan the next day. It was almost impossible to maintain a cool head with the threat of the enemy at our gates. My perception that we were safe flew out the window! Orders came down that we all were to evacuate to Bataan or Corregidor, the tiny island just off the mainland. There was no chance that we could move all our patients, so the unthinkable had to be done: the more seriously injured would be left behind. This action was counter to the Army's usual stance, but the generals knew we hadn't time or transportation to move everyone. I couldn't even look at those men whose fate was left to the enemy. Quite a number of the civilians, including Americans, decided to stay in Manila. The large ex-patriot enclave in the city was comprised of foreigners connected through business such as exporting or oil production. A majority had lived in the Philippines for a decade or more. Some were of the opinion that this imposition would be over in a few weeks, so their exotic lives in the tropics would return to normal. We nurses heard rumors that some American's had even written to General MacArthur, demanding that he provide air transport to the U.S. "as soon as possible." As if he hadn't already tried. When the Army began increasing its troops and weapons in the months proceeding December 7th, those ex-patriots should have thought about leaving on their own.

# CHAPTER 13

ON CHRISTMAS DAY, INSTEAD OF MOUNDS OF turkey with all the trimmings, the hospital staff gladly ate turkey sandwiches, washed down with black coffee or warm beer. Mona didn't finish with surgery until ten o'clock, and was almost too exhausted to eat. After a beer, she revived and insisted on singing Christmas carols until one by one, we all drifted off to check on patients and rest a couple of hours. I couldn't sleep for thinking about Lee, and the days we spent by the ocean. When I wasn't wearing my charm bracelet, it was pinned securely inside my bra; too many valuables were pilfered to take a chance. I fingered the charms, remembering each occasion they were given. As hard as I tried to forget Lee, his face was as familiar as my own.

Just after two a.m., launches started ferrying staff and patients across the bay under the cover of darkness to the refuge of Bataan. At the same time, convoys of trucks left Manila with hundreds of wounded civilians and American soldiers. Other civilians loaded their cars, and in some cases horse carts, with their belongings, and helped jam the only good road onto the peninsula. The Japanese troops had already sent scouts ahead of their main force, who terrorized the unsuspecting passengers by sniping from the tops of palm trees. A company of engineers preceded our evacuation, filling in swampy areas on the Bataan Peninsula where camps were set up.

For decades logging companies tried to strip Bataan of its timber, and fought mosquitoes, dysentery, dengue fever, fungus, and other diseases. The last company pulled out in 1930, leaving behind a wretched jungle where the allied forces were to hold on until Washington sent help. Only isolated little villages existed on that end of the peninsula, and roads were few and unimproved. Refugees slowed the retreat to a crawl, but by the second week of January, 1942, over 100,000 souls inhabited the area.

We expected to find some buildings to use as hospitals; however, there were only a couple of old plantation mansions and primitive sheds. We broke into teams to tackle cleaning some of the sheds, erecting several huge tents, and preparing a surgical theater. Tents were cleaner than any of the buildings in that jungle, since mould and rot claimed all surfaces. Mona was indispensable with her skills of organization, barking orders, and anticipating what was to come. The Japanese were crushing the troops assigned to pull up the rear of the retreating column, and those injured swamped the hospital tents before we were even ready. Never in a million years did I imagine such a scene when we were nursing students. I wanted so much to hear a word from my family, but realized that everyone felt the same.

A major development happened after we arrived at Bataan: we were issued tropical-weight uniforms which was a tremendous improvement! Women's underwear was the only thing the quartermaster didn't have on hand. The heat was unbearably oppressing, and we wished for showers with lots of soap and hot water to rid our bodies of the dirt, sweat, and blood that accumulated during our shifts. The best our camp offered was a bucket of clean water at the end of the day, in which we washed our bodies, hair, and underwear. Mona and I kept each other's hair cut short, to lessen the risk of fungal infections or fleas. We had no time or inclination to think about how unattractive we must look.

Right after we arrived at the Bataan camp, a PBY (the most popular seaplane in the war) flew in one night, landing just off-shore from us. The pilot had several bags of U.S. mail destined for Manila, so he knew much of it belonged to Bataan refugees and troops. A detail was put in charge of sorting, and after a day of great anticipation, the hospital staff gathered in a shed to listen to names being called.

"Ivy Reese!" I jumped forward to retrieve two envelopes. With trembling hands I actually began to cry until Mona poked me in the side and motioned for us to step outside of the crowded room.

"Open them, silly! Looks like the fat one is from your Ma!" she said, and I suddenly realized that Mona had no letters of her own to read.

The afternoon's drenching rain began, so we ducked under the thatched eaves of the shed, but so did everyone else. Finally, Mona suggested that we wait until our shifts ended to read in the privacy of our corner in the nurses' tent dormitory.

"Mona McWhirter! Mona, you've got a letter!" called our friend Mabel, as she stepped outside, waving the envelope. Mona's mouth dropped open, and it was my turn to jab her into action.

"Ivy, it's from me own mither!" she exclaimed, lapsing into her childhood brogue. We each tucked the letters into our pockets, and headed to the wards, anxious to finish our shifts. Mona was called into surgery, and I didn't see her again until that evening.

Stripped to our underwear in the sultry, still night, Mona and I sat on the hard cots, devouring the messages from loved ones. I began reading aloud my letter from Ma, and saw that Mona also had tears staining her cheeks. Of course, my family was concerned that I was still in the Philippines, close to the fighting. They watched newsreels in Bend and read newspapers that described General MacArthur as someone who stayed with his men, making the hard decisions. Ma had no idea that our situation was so dire, since she asked if I still enjoyed the dances and formal evenings. I think she assumed the battles were separate from what I was doing. She shared her news about Mr. Atkins, and she knew that Lizzy had already told me. He liked visiting the ranch, and helped with some projects when he could get away from the store. Her hired hand, Red, had made a big difference in keeping up the ranch, especially since Ma purchased a few head of cattle. Ma was afraid that when Red turned eighteen he would enlist in the Army, but declared she'd cross that bridge when it happened. Granny Ellen, Uncle Bob and Aunt Amy were busy with the war effort forming in Oregon, and Aunt Fay's son planned to enlist if the war was still going by summertime. Lizzy added a note to Ma's letter telling me that she had a new boyfriend, and was learning to speak French in school. The winter hadn't been very cold so far and the snowfall was good. Oh, I loved thinking about all the Christmases we spent in that old ranch house, making candy, baking pies, and singing carols.

Mona opened her letter next, and read aloud her mother's brief wish for a happy holiday in the "foreign lands." One of Mona's brothers had just enlisted in the Navy, and her oldest sister's husband joined the Army. Several cousins were moving to Tacoma for jobs in the ship building industry. Mona's mother signed her letter, "come home soon, my girl" which made Mona laugh, which I knew was her effort to keep from crying.

My letter from Tom revealed he was in Iceland, but expected to be somewhere in Europe by springtime. He was the most aware of our dangerous position, and hoped MacArthur could arrange for transports to remove us from the islands soon. Tom had no idea it was too late, just as we hadn't admitted it to ourselves. I wanted to hear something about Lee, but Tom didn't mention him.

Shelling, sniping, barrages, and sorties equaled carnage no matter what we named the onslaught. The nurses had no time to sit and comfort the injured. We ran from stretcher to stretcher, cot to cot, trying to appear in control of each patient's needs, but fooling no one.

The enemy set up a battery with large guns behind the distant hills, and our camp was within range. When they began pounding steadily at our location, we were forced to move. Once again, we loaded patients and supplies in trucks and moved inland where engineers had prepared a site near a small jungle village. A small stream was designated as the nurses' private bathing area every night and some recruits built a privacy screen. What seemed like an insignificant gesture was more appreciated than they'd ever know. Sanitation was handled better in this new location, with more latrines and even private ones built for the nurses. The food supply was holding out, with canned meats or fish on our plates most days. It was rumored that if rescue came before April or May, we would be okay in that regard. The Malinta Tunnel on Corregidor Island held stores that could also feed those trapped souls about the same amount of time.

By the end of January the tented wards were overflowing with injured or disease-ridden soldiers. The medical staff arranged cots and make-shift beds in the open air jungle, with only a canopy of trees and vines over most of them. In some cases, tarps or sheets were strung above the beds to afford some protection from the sun and rain. Although large red crosses were painted on the hospital tents' roofs, enemy planes occasionally strafed the area, with horrible consequences.

Mona asked to be relieved from the surgical tent for awhile. She told me she couldn't bear to see one more arm or leg sawed off and tossed into a barrel of amputated limbs. In a few days, the doctor who specialized in abdominal surgeries asked for her assistance, and Mona dutifully reported. Captain Roberts assigned me to the ward where soldiers with devastating wounds or burns were placed. When the doctors couldn't do anything for them, lacking instruments and specific medications, or if their wounds were simply too horrible, all we could do was administer morphine to ease their pain until they died. I knew the effect of those decisions would stay with the doctors and nurses forever. It was the most helpless I ever felt in my life. The frustration I felt towards some doctors just two months earlier was swept aside; I now had nothing but respect for their dedication.

At night the camps observed total black-out conditions, which meant we tripped among the jungle cots with small flashlights. Often a weak beam of light would illuminate a large rat climbing on a patient; many of the injured troops were unable to get up, away from the pests. Much of our time was spent answering the screams for help when snakes dropped from the trees, monkeys' pilfered personal items, or wild pigs toppled cots. Eventually we nurses gave up our tented dormitory and moved our bedding into smaller tents so the larger one could be used by the surgeons. We were more at risk for malaria, sleeping more or less in the open. Quinine supplies began to be rationed, dosages cut.

Two young army engineers, who came into the medical camp to see how well a friend was recovering from shrapnel wounds, noticed how we were living in the make shift tents. They enlisted a few more buddies, and in no time at all built several tiny bamboo huts. Mona and I pitched our tent inside the shelter for added protection from mosquitoes, but just having a private shelter with a rickety door felt like a million dollars. As a thank you gesture to the young soldiers, Mona bought some fish from a local vendor and talked our cook into broiling them for a special dinner. Those fellows were as homesick as the nurses, but like us, they were fighting the enemy with all their strength. When they found out that Mona and I were from Oregon, all sorts of questions flew at us. One fellow was from Texas, but thought that after the war he'd try the Pacific Northwest for a change of scenery. They all promised to drop by in a few days, but we never saw them again.

A day or so later, at the end of February, Mona and I were changing dressings on a burn patient, who was trying to be very brave. We were working under a small canopy, facing each other, one on each side. I said something to Mona, who didn't answer; when I looked at her, she was staring past me with a startled expression. About the time I asked, "What is it?" a voice behind me simply said, "Ivy."

I turned and saw a tall G.I. in a muddied and tattered uniform, holding his helmet under one arm. In three steps Lee had me in his arms, crushing my body to his, and then kissing me hard as I held onto him.

# CHAPTER 14

SINCE IT WAS OBVIOUS NEITHER OF US were releasing our grips on the other, Captain Roberts stepped up to take over as Mona's helper with our burn patient. With Lee's arm around my shoulders and mine hugging his waist, we scampered down the muddy path to a place beyond the cots. When we stopped under the palms, I couldn't hold back; I bathed Lee's face in kisses as he pulled me against his chest. We couldn't get enough of each other, but finally hot kisses became spoken endearments. I had to know how he found me and why.

"I overheard some fellas talking about the nurses from Oregon, and had to see for myself. It seemed impossible that you could actually be here!" Lee explained. I never dreamed Lee would show up in the same part of the Pacific Ocean as I, much less on the same island, and couldn't keep from weeping with joy at the sight of him.

I had to say the words that burned in my heart, "I thought you'd never want to see me again." For a moment I couldn't get my breath, hurting in my chest with the pain of pent up emotions. "When I didn't hear from you, it was like an ax split me in half," I sobbed. Lee cupped my face in his hands, his eyes brimming with tears, "I was so wrong, Ivy. You are all I ever wanted. I was so stupid!" He kissed me again, pleading, "Please say you forgive me!"

"Oh, Lee, there's nothing to forgive. I knew you'd be shocked... betrayed. Ma and Mona know what happened, but I couldn't keep it from you any longer. I don't know that I'll ever be able to forgive myself for all the hurt I've caused."

He shook his head, and assured me, "You've got to put it behind you, Ivy. You were young and deceived. I don't care what happened all those years ago. What's important now is that we found each other!" He lightly kissed my forehead, moved on to my mouth with a light touch before we realized we had an audience. It felt so good to laugh at ourselves.

We sat together on the trunk of a palm tree felled by bombings, and spent the next hour talking about everything: Tom, Ma, Lee's parents, and our time in the Pacific. Finally, I felt I had to report back to Captain Roberts, so we made our way through the hundreds of cots and men on the ground. Mona grabbed Lee and rocked back and forth in a big hug, laughing and crying all the time. Some of the injured soldiers whistled and clapped, encouraging a kiss. It was a wonderful afternoon, one that I replayed over and over in times to come.

Mona said she would bunk with one of the other nurses, so Lee and I had our own private hut. We were shy of each other, but had no expectations. Stretched out on a straw pallet, wrapped in each other's arms, we slept until daybreak brought the enemies' bombers back.

We grabbed some toast and coffee in the mess tent, and joined Mona under a tree.

"We've got about two hundred casualties comin' soon, after that raid this morning," Mona said, as she left for the surgery tent.

Turning to Lee I asked, "Where will you be tonight?"

"I've got to head back up country. We're building a road for evacuees; I'm needed up there," Lee said, looking at me, searching for approval. I nodded and he added, "If I can, I'll be back tomorrow or the next day."

Lee pulled me close, and we kissed deeply, lovingly, tenderly. I felt the heat from his body through my thin uniform, and craved more of his touch. A soldier walking by whistled, which brought us back to the present and our duties.

I murmured into his chest, "I don't want to lose you again, please come back."

"Nothing can keep me from you, Ivy. I love you so much," I remember Lee saying.

Mercifully, we did manage to see each other often. By the first week of March, Lee and his men were moved to a bridge project closer to the hospital. His men were suffering the ravages of the jungle, especially dysentery and malaria. Infections of the skin and feet brought hundreds more to the hospital, where our supplies had diminished to almost nothing. For a week Lee thrashed about on a cot in a feverish delirium, with painful joints and headaches. Quinine supplies were extremely low, so the medical staff reduced dosages which meant we just used supplies without giving real relief to those down with malaria. The nurses and doctors needed to feel like we were doing something for our patients, but our efforts were frequently futile.

Sufficient food would have alleviated many conditions. Many of the soldiers had lost a quarter of their normal weight since rationing had slashed the amount of protein they received. Bargaining with the local natives wasn't successful any longer since they also lacked enough food. We were just glad we had a good supply of rice. Occasionally fruit showed up in the mess tent, which was careful portioned out. I could savor the taste of one bite of mango all day.

Bombings shook Bataan daily, and with each one, we knew in a short time dozens or even hundreds of casualties would arrive on our doorstep. Hand-to-hand combat on the road to Manila killed many of our soldiers, and sent hundreds of wounded to the operating rooms. We worked to patch up some of the least serious injuries, to send the soldier back into action as soon as possible. I remember arguing with a recuperating soldier that he could not return to his unit with a stitched up abdomen. Those young men, really just boys, were so brave.

On the evening of March 11, 1942 General MacArthur was evacuated with his wife, son, and staff to Australia. It was a dangerous trip for them, so it became obvious that we had no hope for rescue anytime soon. It almost seemed as if we were being abandoned, along with thousands of American troops. Most of the nurses held their feelings close, but we didn't have to say anything to know how everyone felt. General Wainwright was left in charge on Corregidor Island.

The stress of working long hours, witnessing horrible injuries and multitudes of deaths, was beginning to show on the medical staff. When one of the operating room nurses had a nervous breakdown, Mona stepped right up to cover that duty plus her own. We hardly saw each other since she'd moved permanently to another hut so Lee and I could be alone as much as possible.

It broke my heart to see Lee growing thinner each day; I couldn't fathom how he continued to work so hard in the heat and mud, on such small rations. In the evenings after my shift, I'd bathe in the nurses' enclosure, and Lee would arrive still damp from his dip in the river where the bridge was being constructed. After eating a meal of stingy proportions, we'd return to the hut to stretch out on the pallet and talk about our future. We had to believe that we had a future together. One night soon after MacArthur left, Lee said he had a gift for me.

"I've been carrying this with me for a long time," he said, and plucked a tiny silver charm from a corner of his wallet. "I think this will always mean something to both of us."

The tiny U.S. flag was so detailed, even styled with a breezy ripple from an imaginary wind. It was the perfect charm for the bracelet that I wore or carried with me every day.

"Oh, Lee, you are a darling! It's perfect!" I exclaimed.

"You're my girl, Ivy, and I wish I had more to give you," he said while attaching the charm to my bracelet. I felt a magnetism connecting our hearts, and an overwhelming emotion. I knew that I would lay down my life for Lee, so much did I care for him. What was even better was the love I felt from him for me.

It was only a matter of time... and we both knew it... before we'd sleep together. Sleep... we'd already done that in the little hut, but sleeping "together" was what we both wanted, looked forward to and dreamed about, without having discussed it. Still, I was afraid to allow myself this most natural of all intimacies: afraid of disappointing Lee and afraid of giving too much of myself too soon. I think that Lee held back because he didn't want me to think he expected a physical intimacy right away.

A week of unrelenting bombardment flooded the hospital grounds with wounded and dying soldiers. Civilians, including women and children, were brought in on the backs of relatives and soldiers; the enemy forces didn't care who got in the way of their objective. Grievous wounds were especially heartbreaking when observed on tiny bodies, and many a nurse lost her composure when there was no hope of saving the little patient. I wondered whether I could ever forget the devastation and suffering of the last three months. The doctors and nurses worked so hard to mend the injured, only to see many of them succumb to secondary infections, mostly due to the unsanitary conditions beyond our control. Packaged sterile bandages were a thing of the past, so the little group of nuns from the Manila school began boiling old ones for re-use. Water in and around the hospital was polluted except for one deep well, but the pump was temperamental. We boiled all water used for cooking and drinking, and still worried about contamination. Runoff from the frequent rains polluted the bathing stream so it was no longer safe to use it. We were back to washing up in a bucket of water, boiled and cooled.

I got a message from Lee that part of their bridge work had been destroyed in a bombing, and they were working day and night to finish the repair. A few days later an officer arrived at the hospital, wounded in sniper fire near Lee's bridge. He told me that several G.I.'s had been killed, but knew nothing about Lee. That night Mona found me slumped beside our hut, sobbing because I couldn't find out where Lee was.

"Mona, I can't live without him! You just don't know what Lee means to me!" I cried.

"I do know, Ivy. Just have faith that he will be here as soon as he can. Trust Lee, Ivy, and be brave," she said, wrapping her arms around my shoulders.

As usual, Mona was right. I had to believe he wasn't hurt, and began telling myself that he had been unavoidably detained. A few days later he casually walked back into my life, as if he'd been gone just a few hours. A bandage was wrapped around his forehead, but he brushed aside any help.

"Miss me?" he grinned, as he walked toward me through the rows of injured troops.

Spinning around to face him, I emotionally said, "Couldn't you have sent word that you were alright? I thought the worst!"

"Oh, Honey, I'm sorry. I had to take a truck to get more supplies down along the coast. The roads were so bad we had a tough time getting back. I sent word with a corpsman that I'd be gone awhile. I guess you didn't get that."

I wrapped my arms around him, and sobbed that I never wanted him to leave me.

"I love you, Lee, more than I ever thought possible. If something happens to you, I'll never be happy again," I confessed. He smiled and just replied, "There's only one thing to do, Ivy." I stepped back and looked questioningly at him.

My love dropped to one knee; under the tattered palm trees and with the sounds of distant bombing, he asked me to marry him that very day, that very hour.

Just as if we were at home in Fort Rock, after a dance at the Grange, watching the stars rotate around the night sky, he took my hand. I answered, "Yes, I will marry you, Lee."

# CHAPTER 15

MONA AND MABEL WERE ASSIGNED THE TASK of locating a chaplain who would agree to perform a ceremony with so little notice, while Lee washed up and borrowed a clean uniform. I left my dress uniform behind when we evacuated Manila; however one of my fellow nurses was kind enough to lend me her clean khaki blouse and skirt. With some strategically pinned tucks, my wedding attire was complete. Lee and I helped each other pin on our lieutenant bars; we were ready.

Mona led us to a village chapel which had barely survived numerous bombing strikes, where an army chaplain arranged his vestments. Some of our friends heard about this hastily planned wedding, and banded together as our witnesses. Lee and I cared only for the brief words that would link us forever. With my hand cupped in his, I felt Lee tremble; our eyes met while the chaplain pronounced us "husband and wife" and I saw his tears matched mine. While enemy fire boomed in the background, we were blessed in our union, kissed each other, and were handed a handwritten certificate that our chaplain said "should convince the U.S. government we were legally married." He also had us stand in front of the chapel so he could snap a photo and promised to get a copy to me some day. The whole ceremony lasted about five minutes.

Afterwards, I had to return to the wards for a few hours, while Lee disappeared on a mysterious task. When I got off duty and hurried down the path towards the little hut, Lee intercepted me.

"Well, Mrs. Johnson, will you accompany me to our honeymoon suite?" he said. I thought he was joking about our ramshackle hut, but he steered me towards one of the old plantation mansions, recently used as battalion headquarters. A captain assigned to duty there gave up his private room for the night, just for us. I've always thought that it was a wonderfully thoughtful gesture, given what kind of stress that officer was under.

Mable arrived carrying a dinner tray for the honeymooners, complete with canned salmon chunks in a white sauce, noodles, and fresh fruit. She never disclosed who provided the salmon. Captain Roberts didn't want to see me until the next afternoon, and said I should not even think about the hospital until then.

Our first night together as man and wife was all and more than we imagined. We were shy, and yet anxious to know each other completely. There wasn't much we didn't already know about each other except this heavenly gift. What began with slowly undressing each other, escalated quickly into caressing and making our bodies touch from lips to toes. Lee murmured, "I've waited so long, Ivy," and we became one. We cried in our happiness, laughed at our impatience, and promised that the next time we wouldn't be rushed. Of course, it was a promise we couldn't keep. That night was replayed over and over in my dreams, in the years to come.

We married on March 31, 1942, and on April 8 nurses were ordered to prepare for evacuation to the Malinta Tunnel on Corregidor. The enemy was overrunning the towns and villages, and it was only a matter of a few days before Bataan would fall. A few nurses were chosen to escape on a PBY that flew in, dodging flak in the darkness. Captain Roberts and her next in command decided who should leave. They chose mostly older women who might not survive an extended internment, if it came to that. I gave one of them a letter for Ma, telling her I was okay, and hoped to be back in the states soon. A letter from home would have meant so much to me, and I was certain Ma had written, but I had to be satisfied reading her last letter over and over. I wished these nurses good luck as they departed before dawn for Australia, and held my breath until the plane was beyond the range of the guns across the bay.

Lee's engineers were pulled off bridge work, and joined with the regular troops, repelling the enemy as long as possible. He confided to me that they would certainly be taken prisoner, but he had confidence in General King's staff to negotiate terms for humane treatment of the troops. He hoped that if Corregidor fell, our medical staff would be turned over to a Red Cross unit.

Having seen all angles of his thin frame, I worried how he would survive in a prison camp.

He tried to reassure me, by joking "I'm just at my fighting weight, Ivy. Don't worry, I doubt if the war will last much longer anyway." Neither of us believed that, but I pretended to agree so the subject wouldn't loom over our last few hours together. We had one more night alone in our little bamboo hut. We talked about plans following the war, and he asked if I would mind being married to a part-time rancher. Lee was proud of his engineering career, but I wasn't surprised that he dreamed of being on the land again. I guess it was in my blood too, since the memory of the smell of our barn and the sound of bawling calves made me smile in the dark.

"I wish I had a ring for you, Ivy. You deserved a real wedding with all the trimmings."

I quickly quieted his regrets, "Lee, I have my charm bracelet, and I'll keep it close to my heart always. Every time I look at an individual charm, I remember when you gave it to me, and what it stands for. We'll have time later to celebrate our marriage with families back home." We made love one more time, and the next day all of the remaining nurses were transported to Corregidor.

We were ordered to leave the non-ambulatory patients behind, but at the last minute there was a scramble to load many of them on the barges that navigated the narrow channel to Corregidor. Waiting as long as I dared to board, Lee and I embraced, whispering endearments and wiping each other's tears away. I impulsively wanted to wail and tear out my hair, being separated just after finding each other; however, most all of the medical staff on the barge had their own anguish to hold in check. As Captain Roberts said, we nurses had to maintain a calm attitude, to reassure everyone else.

Everyone, civilians and Army personnel, arrived safely on Corregidor, and were met by soldiers who had been stationed there for several months. I personally appreciated a safe place to sleep and the best food we'd eaten in months. The 800 feet long Malinta Tunnel was built years earlier, fortified with concrete, and stocked with tons of food and water. Medical supplies were abundantly available in a small operating theater off the main tunnel, and there were beds for 1,000 casualties. It was truly a masterpiece of planning, and at first I liked the idea of having a burrow in which to retreat.

Word came from General Wainwright that Bataan fell the day after we left, and troops there were forced to surrender. What happened next went down in history as the vilest treatment of POW's in World War II. Seventy thousand American and Filipino soldiers were marched sixty miles to disembarkation points, where they were shipped to various prisons and work camps. On that Bataan Death March, one-fourth of the soldiers died under terrible circumstances, and many more died in captivity. I tried not to think about Lee's fate; my friends and I spoke only of seeing him again once the war was over. We worked long hours, which were a godsend, since it kept my mind busy, not dwelling on personal concerns. Only occasionally I'd retreat into a dark corner of a tunnel, have a good cry, and then return to duty.

Although Malinta Tunnel was deep inside a rocky hill, we could hear and feel the concussions from bombs dropped or shelling from big guns on the mainland. Mona was assigned to the surgery unit once more, and she told me they soon hardly flinched at the sounds and vibrations. After a couple of weeks, being cooped up deep underground began to eat at me. I joined a group that stepped outside the tunnel's entrance in the protection of darkness, and we relaxed in the fresh air and socialized like young people do everywhere. One evening I got Mona to join me, and she entertained us by singing a heartfelt "*Somewhere over the Rainbow*." A lieutenant from New York was determined to see more of Mona, and surprisingly, she welcomed his attention.

Over the next couple of weeks they met most evenings outside the tunnel, and sometimes they strolled a little distance from the tunnel's entrance to find a quiet corner to talk. It was dangerous, however many couples secretly met in the shadows outside the protective tunnel. Captain Roberts seemed to turn a blind eye to the escapades; the soldiers and nurses were so young, and life was unsure. One night when we were kept deep in the hospital tunnel with a flood of injuries following a day of an incessant barrage from the big guns, a huge explosion rocked the tunnel. I thought the roof was going to collapse on us. Although it held firm, waves of concrete dust blinded everyone, and I felt my lungs revolt against the caustic particles breathed in. We ran into the more protected lateral tunnels to reach clean air, and grabbed surgical masks before helping our patients in the same way. Soon, reports trickled into the wards that a bomb had exploded right at the Malinta Tunnel entrance, and the injured began arriving on stretchers. Corpsmen who rushed to the scene told us the fatalities numbered over one hundred. Mona's face blanched.

"Matt said he would meet me there tonight," she said, so quietly I could barely hear.

Mona and I rushed from one cot to another as the injured were brought to triage, all the while looking at the faces of each, searching for Matt.

It was the next day before one of his friends came to Mona with the sorrowful news of Matt's instantaneous death in the bombing.

Mona stood in silence for a minute, then "I'm glad he didn't suffer, like so many of these poor guys…" she said, waving her hand toward the hundreds of wounded soldiers, many who wouldn't survive. Later she told me that she'd been wrong to break her own rule about falling in love with a G.I.

Mona's loss reminded me of how fragile our lives were, and I wondered if I would know in my heart if Lee had been killed. I wanted to know if he was still alive, but didn't want to have a confirmation that he was dead. Every night I lulled myself to sleep by remembering the sweet days and nights we spent together, before and after our marriage. Nothing could take those memories away.

A large number of our patients were civilians representing many different nationalities, caught in the wrong place at the wrong time. Filipinos who were injured usually had their families by their sides, which helped our workloads. However, it meant they also depended on us to shelter and feed them. Food supplies were being depleted faster than planned, and there was no way to restock. The Japanese blockade of Corregidor's coast effectively prevented the movement of civilian aid from other islands. By the end of April, rumors were rampant that General Wainwright would surrender the Philippines.

General MacArthur was quoted as telling Wainwright to hold on at all cost, but he was safe in Australia.

Water rationing was imposed, which meant the laundry stopped washing sheets and blankets. We no longer washed our clothes; instead we rinsed out our underwear in the same gallon of water used to wash our bodies each evening. Patients and staff alike began to suffer skin infections and rashes that would have healed with cleaner practices. On top of that, nurses were beleaguered with malarial fevers and dysentery, which put many of us in bed for days at a time. Doctors worked miracles in surgery, while barely able to stand upright themselves.

On the evening of May 4th, several nurses began stuffing bags with their personal belongings, and quickly followed an officer out of the tunnel. Later we learned that a submarine had surfaced in the bay, with instructions to evacuate a few nurses. Once again, Captain Roberts made the hard decision of who could leave, and we heard that two of the chosen nurses had refused to go. Some nurses wept in despair when they saw others escaping to safety, however I felt nothing but gladness for them. At least, staying in the Philippines kept me closer to Lee. I held out hope that the war would end soon and. we would be reunited.

The next morning General Wainwright walked through the tunnel, stopping to shake hands with patients and staff. We listened as he thanked us for our service and dedication, and then we knew he was going to surrender the island.

The dreaded invasion took place quickly the next day, with surprisingly little resistance. Suddenly about twenty Japanese soldiers stomped into Malinta Tunnel, with the officers barking orders at the doctors. We were allowed to keep a few corpsmen on staff, but combat soldiers were transported to prison camps. Civilians and bedridden troops were allowed to stay for the time being. Mona, Mabel, and I stood shoulder to shoulder along the tunnel wall, frightened of the cold look on the enemies' faces. When an officer stopped at a wounded G.I.'s bed and threw back the sheet to see his condition, a doctor objected and moved to stop what was happening. In a split second, the enemy officer struck him across the face, and yelled to move away or be shot. It became clear we no longer controlled our lives. Foolishly, we held out hope that the hospital staff would be turned over to the Red Cross as non-combatants.

# CHAPTER 16

IT TOOK ONLY TWO DAYS TO REALIZE we wouldn't be leaving the Philippines with the Red Cross or anyone else. We were allowed to continue treating patients, especially after the enemy officers saw that the staff had taken good care of their injured soldiers taken prisoner by our troops. Not long after the invasion, everyone in the tunnel was moved outside, and the fresh air was a godsend! We had become so accustomed to the stale, polluted air in the tunnel that it was almost intoxicating to breathe the salty air blowing off the beach. Being out of the tunnel presented new challenges such as protecting the patients and staff from mosquitoes and other pests. We scrounged netting from all sources, and it still was not enough. Captain Roberts insisted that the hospital staff take care of our own needs first, since we had to stay in good health to care for the others.

Finding food was an immediate concern for the hundreds of patients and workers for every meal, every day. Our captors provided a bare minimum of rations for those who worked, and even less for those who were bedridden. Without food to help their bodies heal, patients began dying in great numbers.

Mona was particularly affected by the deaths of the little Filipino children, who came to us with injuries or diseases, and suffered further from lack of enough food. I believe she was thinking about her brothers and sisters still at home when she looked into the eyes of our tiny patients. I watched as her backbone grew stiffer, and her jaw more determined; she hadn't sung in weeks, but she never cried. Our personal losses were mounting, and I had to admit that the only thought that kept me going was seeing Lee again.

An American woman, who had come to the Philippines with her husband ten years earlier, was one of my patients. Her husband died in one of the first attacks on Manila, and her grown children lived in the states. The doctor managed to relieve her dengue fever symptoms, but Lydia seemed reluctant to leave.

"Can I stay and help you?" she begged. "I know a little about hospitals and nursing, so I think I'd not be in the way."

"I'd love to have your help, but let me check with Captain Roberts," I replied hopefully.

Lydia took over a large children's ward with volunteers she solicited from her own acquaintances trapped on Corregidor. They became an integral unit of the hospital and operated as well as most of the other wards. Mona went back to assisting the surgeons and over time she regained some of her old self.

The heat and rain could turn a normal day into a steaming nightmare. Tarps strung over beds were so tattered by then that the rain streamed onto the patients. The sun was so hot and unforgiving we gave palm leaf fronds to patients to shield their eyes. Corregidor was stripped of trees and shrubs after the intense bombings. The Japanese commandant allowed two of our corpsmen to gather fronds from the jungle across the bay, with an armed escort of course. That small addition to our bag of remedies went a long way providing comfort for the hundreds under our care.

Rice was our daily fare for two meals a day, sometimes decorated with a few specks of canned tomatoes. I craved something sweet all of the time. In the evenings, after our sparse scoop of rice, Mona and I reminisced about Granny Ellen's cakes and pies, fried chicken, and pot roast with all the trimmings. It did us absolutely no good to torture each other with made up menus for holidays or Sunday dinners, but it passed the time and we enjoyed talking about home. Sometimes we'd plan in detail the party for our reunion when the war ended, and named everyone who would come.

On July 2$^{nd}$ Captain Robertson announced that all medical personnel were being sent to Manila. The Japanese commandant assured the doctors that medical facilities would be available, with better food, and dormitories for the staff. No one would answer our questions about the fate of our patients. Our rotting old freighter that rolled its way up Manila Bay also held selected civilians, including some Americans. We had been lulled into looking forward to this move, not aware of its consequences.

Upon arrival in Manila, the doctors and corpsmen were herded into trucks as we were held back to travel in a separate conveyance. Our destination was Santo Tomas Internment Camp, but the men were spread out among several prisons in the Philippines. Some of our nurses began weeping, but I could only stand there, stunned. I looked at Mona, who gave me a half-smirk.

"I'm not surprised, are you?" she asked, not really expecting an answer.

By late afternoon we entered the gates of Santo Tomas, our home for the duration of the war. It was originally built as a university on about sixty acres of land enclosed by a tall fence, and presently guarded by sentries. At first glance, it looked like a peaceful expanse of green lawn with many buildings to house internees. On closer inspection, we found that the camp was already filled with almost 4,000 civilians from all walks of life, deemed enemies of Japan. A board representing the internees served as a liaison with the commandant. The board in turn formed committees to manage the mini-city within its walls. I admired the attempt to maintain a semblance of a regular city government in the midst of such hardship. Most of what the committees handled related to food and housing; realistically, the board had little clout with our captors.

We reunited with acquaintances from the beautiful days before the December attacks. Whole families were interned in some cases, but many had been separated. With part of the family living outside the walls, usually a spouse petitioned (to deaf ears) for release from the camp. Right away we learned to hastily bow from the waist to Japanese officers who approached or spoke to us. An infraction of this rule could bring a club down on your head or back. Every morning at seven o'clock sharp, all internees had to assemble for "tenko," or roll call. No matter what we were doing, this had to be obeyed, or suffer the consequences.

The dormitory that was promised to the nurses was simply an old classroom already in use by other internees, so crowded that we slept touching each other on all sides. The food provided was riddled with worms and bugs, so we learned how to purchase fruits, breads, and cereals from local vendors who were allowed to come inside the entrance and set up shop. Many internees tended small gardens, and sold what they didn't need for themselves. Most of us still had money and jewelry hidden on us or with our belongings. Without that re-source, we'd have been in worse condition than we were already.

Most of the internees had been in Santo Tomas several months by then, and knew the ropes. If a person were lucky enough to have a friend or family outside the walls, food could arrive every "package day." It was difficult to get enough of the right foods to keep our bodies from wasting away. Given the condition I was in already after the siege on Corregidor, I'm not sure how I kept upright. It must have been pure determination! Mona suffered from open sores on the soles of her feet and palms of her hands. Mabel and I finally convinced her to stay on her cot, and we took care of her for a change. The building we slept in still had running water, but the one bathroom on our floor meant there was always a long line for its use. Since Mona couldn't stand up, she used a chamber pot that we could empty on our turns in the bathroom. We carried Mona to the parade grounds and supported her between us for roll call. Finally after a couple of vitamin shots, salves, and fish for one meal a day, Mona's sores healed over, and she was welcomed into the working population.

All nurses were assigned a four-hour shift in the hospital building, which sapped the little strength we did have. Several American civilian doctors trapped in Manila were interned in Santo Tomas to work in the hospital, setting bones, performing surgeries, and overseeing our care for burn victims. Our work was continually interrupted by Japanese officers walking through the wards, since we were expected to stop and bow, or suffer punishment. There was no consistency in the punishments; sometimes a small breach in the rules would elicit a flogging, whereas something major might even be overlooked. I think the uncertainty is what kept everyone scared.

Rumor was that the Army doctors and other male Corregidor staff were being held in Bilibid Prison, a particularly cruel pest hole. One of the Catholic priests volunteered to be a secret courier between the prison and Santo Tomas nurses, so we methodically sent medicines and small amounts of food when available. Some brave nurses actually joined the Philippine resistance movement, risking certain death if they were discovered.

Overcrowding inside the buildings drove hundreds outdoors during the days. Our captors demanded that all internees spend the nights inside; however, they turned a blind eye when little shacks, much like our huts on Bataan, started showing up. Mona, Mabel, and

I pilfered scraps of wood, cardboard, fabric...anything that would shut out the sun and give a semblance of privacy. The six by six structure wasn't tall enough for us to stand up straight, but there was room for the three of us to sit and relax. The sides rolled up to allow a cooling breeze, and we called the shack our "beach house."

The "Sanitation Committee" formed a crew to dig latrines since the indoor bathrooms couldn't accommodate the overcrowded camp. Captain Roberts asked for two nurses to make recommendations for the most hygienic arrangement. I suggested that toilet seat lids be added to keep the flies at a minimum, and the art teacher offered to paint signs to remind everyone to keep the lids closed.

Having our own garden seemed a good idea, except that finding the time for tending the little vegetables was hindered by the pressure of our patients' needs. I bargained for some seeds to get started, and for once I appreciated the frequent rain showers. Mona and Mabel weren't raised on a farm, so they gladly made me "chief gardener," but both were good about helping me weed between the rows when the time came. Squash and tomatoes were our best producers; however, a slower crop of strange root vegetables were appreciated too. Of course, our harvest was small, but it added variety to an otherwise tasteless diet, and greens important to our health. Some days, when I had my hands in the soil, I'd have a flashback to Ma's big garden plot and smile at nothing in particular.

One morning in October I was about to sign off my shift when down the hall I heard, "Ivy! Ivy!" and looked up to see our friend Lydia running towards me. For the previous three months she had been held in a Catholic chapel in Manila, but it was being cleared for wounded Japanese soldiers. I approached one of the more likeable guards and obtained permission for Lydia to house with us, and got her a job in the hospital. Mona and Mabel agreed that we should include Lydia at the beach house. The close friendship that the four of us nurtured helped maintain the hope required to stay alive.

Lydia's life before moving to Manila in the early 1930's was in sharp contrast to the rest of us. She grew up in a privileged household, much like the one where Mona had worked as a young woman. After graduating from an Ivy League university, Lydia worked for a publishing company until she met and married Bill. They relished the exotic places Bill's job took them, and had two children along the way. Both of their sons were attending college in California, and Lydia was thankful for that. She had been able to get letters to them through Filipino contacts in the city, and offered to get our letters out of the country too. The three of us immediately retreated to a corner of the beach house to write a one-page letter to our families. I wrote in vague terms of our internment, not letting on how serious our situation was. I knew Ma and Lizzy were worried enough, so I wrote mostly about the nursing duties. I said nothing about Lee being marched off when Bataan fell because I knew they'd assume the worst. Reading the news of our reconciliation and marriage would have to be enough at that time.

Lydia confided that filling her time with hospital duties was a godsend, and kept her from dwelling on Bill's death. I could tell that they had a special partnership in their marriage, and dreamed of the same for Lee and me.

The months dragged on with a daily struggle to stay dry, fed, and healthy. Although Santo Tomas grounds were sixty acres, our captors restricted our movements to the area around the main buildings. With so many bodies enclosed in the small area, disease and infections were impossible to control. Most were treated as outpatients, with the more serious admitted to the hospital. The doctors had few medicines for treating the worst cases, so we lost many of those patients. Incessant rains, every day during the autumn, added to our misery. None of us had adequate clothing or bedding until Lydia's friends in the city brought a box containing a water repellant poncho and a blanket for each of us four gals.

A relapse of malaria put me in bed for almost two weeks, my worst episode yet. It left me even weaker than before, and for awhile I was in a dark place, mentally. Mona's energy and downright badgering forced me to quit feeling sorry for myself.

Christmas 1942: Red Santa costumes, cut out snowflakes, decorated trees, manger scene, and candy, all to make a real holiday for the children in camp. Everyone worked together to make dolls for the girls and wooden trucks for the boys. For some girls in their teens, the nurses searched through the few cosmetics we still owned. I believe the worn down lip sticks and scant pots of rouge were the biggest hits of all. The commandant allowed internees to sing Christmas carols, organized by the Santo Tomas Entertainment Committee. For almost 4,000 people cooped up together, tired of the same old faces and complaints, the evening was magical and full of love. More than ever, we felt the need to pull together and stay alive until rescue.

# CHAPTER 17

ON NEW YEAR'S DAY, 1943, LYDIA'S FRIENDS surprised us on package day with a cooked turkey, vegetables, and a whole raisin pie. Mona took on the duty of carving the big bird into thin slices, so we could share the succulent meat with the medical staff. No turkey since then has ever tasted so good!

While treating a young man in the hospital, I felt I had seen him before. About the time I started to ask him, he said to me, "Are you Lt. Lee Johnson's wife?"

Startled, because that was the first time I'd been referred to that way, I replied, "Yes, I am, and how you know me?"

"I was at the old chapel when you got married. I'm Private Carter," he said, smiling broadly. "Did you ever get word from the Captain after the Japs took us away?"

"No! Do you know anything? How did you get away?" I implored him.

"I was with him on that march north; we kinda helped each other along and made it to the port. I gotta tell you, lots of our guys died along that road, and I saw things I never want to think about again." He turned his face aside, embarrassed of the sobs that quickly escaped his throat. I gently wiped his face with a damp cloth, waiting.

"We heard about it, and I've been frantic about Lee, and well, you all," I told him.

"I was lucky. Two other guys and I slipped away one night near the port, knowing we didn't have much chance of dodging the patrols. We made it though, got separated, and since I'm small-like and was so tanned from the sun, I found...well, stole...some civilian clothes and a big hat, and passed as a local for awhile. Finally, somebody figured out I wasn't Filipino, and threw me in Santo Tomas, thinking I was an American oil worker. If they knew I was a soldier, I'd be shot right away," he said, in a low voice.

"Do you know where the Japanese were taking Lee and the rest of the men?" I asked, choking with the words.

"Well, there was talk that a ship was hauling several hundred of our soldiers straight to Japan. I guess they need mine workers real bad," he said.

It was hard to hear that Lee might be in Japan, but then again, at least I knew he survived the march from Bataan.

Private Carter added, "Lt. Johnson talked about you a lot, and said he would make it through somehow, because you two had a lot of plans back in Oregon."

I broke down crying, after trying so hard to stay composed. That poor soldier didn't know what to do with me, and finally he asked if I would help keep his secret in camp. Of course, I agreed that no one needed to know of his deception, and I shuddered to think of what would happen if our captors found out.

I shared the information about Lee with my three friends, and they understood when I said I couldn't disclose the bearer of the news. Lee was alive, I was sure of it in 1943! In 1944 I wasn't so sure any more.

For awhile I let myself think about our last few nights together, trying to relive the feelings of tenderness and passion. After a week of crying myself to sleep every night, I decided nothing was to be gained by the dreamy reminiscing all of the time. I volunteered to work extra hours in the hospital which exhausted me enough that sleep came quickly. It seems silly to think about now, but I assigned Sunday night as my "thinking about Lee" time. Anytime I felt like I was slipping into despair over our situation in camp, I'd remind myself that on Sunday I could think about Lee. In essence I gave myself permission to delay being depressed. On clear nights when I was on duty and the patients slept, I sat in the doorway to watch the stars. I pretended that Lee and I were looking at the same heavenly bodies at the same time. When a shooting star streaked across the black expanse, I had to believe that he saw it too.

Depression was one of the sicknesses no one wanted to talk about, however badly most of us were affected. Nurses were supposed to watch the patients for signs of depression, since giving up mentally sapped the ability of the body to heal physically. The medical staff certainly suffered breakdowns, but we had little time to rest and recover. In our years of imprisonment, only two nurses became totally debilitated, requiring long durations of bed rest. None of us looked upon those cases with anything but concern; we all realized that any of us could be next.

One particularly steamy July afternoon, when Mona and I were resting in the beach house, a young Filipino boy came to me with a note. A priest named Father Manuel, who ministered to the Catholic population in Santo Tomas, asked me to meet him in a secluded room off the chapel. It all sounded so secretive, I wondered why he sought me out.

Father Manuel was an old man, clearly worn down by the war and his responsibilities. When he should have been enjoying semi-retirement, sitting under a tree with little children at his feet, he was instead fighting to keep human beings of all faiths alive until Manila was liberated. He explained that he needed someone as an undercover courier between Santo Tomas and a large cathedral across town. He was not allowed to leave the camp any longer, but could get permission from the commandant allowing me to go twice a week with the excuse of treating nuns sick with malaria. Father Manuel said he regularly received information about movements of Japanese ships, and his job was to get these reports to a contact at the cathedral. I wasn't told where it would go from there. It was dangerous, of course; however I was eager to do anything to stall the enemy. I told myself that this contribution might somehow get Lee home sooner. Hidden under a bandage on my arm or ankle were coded messages informing the allies of up to date strategy planned by the Japanese. When I was searched before exiting Santo Tomas' gate, usually any bag I carried was dumped on the ground. The Japanese were accustomed to seeing everyone with infections or wounds, so they usually didn't look twice at the bandages covering different parts of my body. There was a close call one afternoon, when a new guard demanded that I remove the bandage around my forearm. At first I pretended to not understand his order. When he began screaming in my face, another guard stepped up and speaking in English, he told me to take the bandage off. I pointed to a red spot showing just above the soiled bandage, and said "Staph infection, very bad!" He jumped back, exclaiming, "Kitai!" The other guard quickly moved away, and I was allowed to pass. Following that incident, my exit through the gate proceeded without delay. For five months this operation was carried out like clockwork, until the commandant decided that the nuns were getting too much attention, and terminated my visits to the cathedral. I didn't ask Father Manuel who became his next courier; the less I knew, the less I could be forced to tell if my involvement were discovered.

Santo Tomas had many heroes who performed their own missions, however small. Medicines were smuggled in, and letters smuggled out. Children kept up with school work through dedicated teachers; black market food helped keep bodies functioning (barely); a recreation committee made certain that musicals and games were on the calendar often enough to keep spirits up. Small kindnesses happened every day, and without those we would have been as bad off as the prisoners in Bilibid: existing without hope.

An American woman who was a retired teacher from Florida formed a children's art club; she called it "Art for the Heart." There was an exhibit after a few weeks which inspired Mabel so much that she sent out a survey to determine how many adult internees were interested in organizing an "Artist Colony." The results were overwhelmingly in favor of offering classes in water color, sculpture, pottery, and sketching. Mabel enlisted the help of some very talented instructors, while she used her organizational skills in locating supplies for their classes. She even met with the Japanese commandant in charge of Santo Tomas, and convinced him that keeping internees busy with activities kept insurrection at bay. Following the meeting, she was allowed to submit a list of needed supplies each week, which were delivered in time for the classes. I'm sure local shopkeepers were persuaded to "donate" these items.

On one sunny morning I got a whiff of newly cut grass from beyond the camp's wall. I wondered who could care about trimming grass at this time. The aroma stayed with me all day, and kept reminding me of the ranch and my family. So many summer evenings we would sit outdoors and take in the perfume of cut grass from the surrounding ranches, or ozone in the air from the distant lightening. I wondered whether Fort Rock was getting the rain Ma needed to sustain our ranch. Ironically, Santo Tomas got too much and Fort Rock never had enough.

Lydia began suffering from terrible dysentery and malarial fever, and then Mabel followed right behind with her own problem, an obstructed bowel. After several attempts to unblock Mabel's bowel with conventional methods, Mona applied a warm castor oil compress to her abdomen, then gently massaged the area. After two days of this treatment, the obstruction moved and there was no lasting damage to Mabel's bowels. No matter how hard we tried, the healthy foods our bodies needed were just not available in quantity. Lydia stayed in bed a few days, but when the worst of the dysentery was over, she went back to work bent over and shaky. Our second crop of vegetables finally ripened, so our diet improved somewhat.

About this time the commandant decided the medical staff wasn't required to attend tenko. However, he declared a new restriction on package days, by allowing only one every two weeks. He also cut in half the number of local vendors permitted inside the walls. While I was still acting as a courier to the cathedral across the city, I could quickly buy a few ounces of food before returning to Santo Tomas. The cash to buy these items had become scarce, although the four of us pooled all our resources. On an afternoon that found all of us resting in the beach house, we had to admit we were down to relying on rations provided by our captors, however insufficient and disgusting they were.

"Wait! I have something that will help," I said, unpinning the silver charm bracelet from my tattered bra. "I'll use one of the charms to buy as much as I can talk a vendor out of!"

"No you won't!" Mona said. "Your bracelet stands in for a wedding band, and none of us will let you sell it."

I shook my head, "But Mona, even if it were a ring, Lee would want us to trade it for food."

Lydia declared that after the war she would personally replace every charm we used. I had a difficult time deciding which charm would come off first, but Mona suggested that I start with the most recent one Lee gave me, the American flag.

When I showed it to a vendor the next morning, he offered me just a loaf of brown bread; however, an older woman who had dried meats hanging from cane poles, offered two pieces. I bargained with her to get four pieces of the stringy meat and a bag of dried beans. Back at the beach house, we decided to stretch the meat into meals for four days by cooking one piece with beans. It was heavenly! Just a few weeks earlier, Dr. Carlisle showed Mona how to assemble parts to build a small stove in the beach house. Having a way to cook meals meant that we could buy dried foods at lower prices than having to buy foods cooked by the vendors. It was a good feeling to know just exactly what was in our soups and porridge. Mona suggested that we buy a crate of fruit to slice and dry in the sizzling weather. Spurred by the donation of my silver charm, Lydia remembered she had a sapphire ring, which prompted oh's and ah's from the three of us when she brought the dazzler out of hiding.

"Would it be best to sell it for cash, rather than trade for food?" Lydia asked.

"I suspect we'd gain more by doing it that way, if we can find a buyer," Mona said. "Can your friends in the city help?"

"I can ask!" Lydia said. The note she smuggled out was answered in a few hours, to our surprise.

"Carlos says he will try to sell it to one of his business acquaintances! On the next package day, he'll show up with some food in a sack, and when we shake hands, I'll slip him the ring."

Mona asked what we'd all been thinking, "How much do you think he'll get for it?"

"I paid over a hundred dollars for the ring in 1935, but I'd be happy to get fifty today," Lydia admitted.

Mabel countered, "Even thirty." And we all nodded.

Three weeks later Lydia had twenty-five dollars in her hands. We were so excited, and were tempted to be extravagant for the first time in two years; however, that money was tightly held and wisely spent.

We knew there were two radios in Santo Tomas, secretly built and ingeniously hidden. Occasionally news circulated regarding where the allies were fighting, battles won, and enemy ships destroyed. Seldom was there mention of our losses. I understood that some messages were sent out from Santo Tomas regarding our desperate situation. The Red Cross attempted to deliver food parcels to the camp, after hearing of our plight, but most of the time the commandant turned them away.

A large number of the nurses were suffering from illnesses associated with vitamin deficiencies and parasites. We were short-staffed to begin with, and when several nurses couldn't stay on their feet, much less work, the rest of us pulled double shifts day after day. Mona worked four hours in surgery, then four more in the wards. Mabel and I took the early morning shift in the wards, then another shift helping patients who were spread out among the trees. An order from the Japanese commandant had relaxed the restriction on time spent in the shacks; therefore many internees abandoned their cramped pallets in the stone buildings for more privacy and uninterrupted sleep. There was an added danger of sleeping in the scattered shacks, since women were more vulnerable to attacks by the guards. During our internment, civilian women were raped or beaten several times, but we learned to not even report these incidences to the commandant. Army nurses had been spared, but we always made sure none of us were alone in the beach house after dark; all internees were encouraged to practice this deterrent to attacks.

Each doctor assigned to patients living outdoors walked up and down the paths, followed by a nurse who carried miscellaneous drugs, bandages, and clean water. Dirt invaded every bed, and patients suffered from insect bites, sunburn, and painful bed sores no matter how hard we tried.

Mona was frequently assigned to assist Dr. Carlisle in surgery; in fact, she seemed to be his first choice on particularly complicated cases. Mona considered him especially skilled on facial reconstructions, using new techniques he brought to the hospital from his residency in New York City. Many of the internees were still suffering from injuries sustained in the initial bombing of Manila. Considering that Dr. Carlisle had no access to the latest equipment and drugs, what he accomplished was nothing short of a miracle. Mona told us that he took the job in the Philippines in 1939, volunteering with a medical group that performed surgeries for the poor population in Manila.

In November, just when I was thinking our patient load couldn't get any worse, a catastrophic event pushed the medical staff to the limit.

# CHAPTER 18

WEATHER IN THE PHILIPPINES, FROM MAY THROUGH November, can be described in two ways: hot and wet, and then hot and very wet! I remember how we suffered through our training in south Texas, with the heat and humidity. That was nothing compared with the misery we endured in Santo Tomas. Mona said she felt like a Christmas pudding: steamed, inside and out. No wonder the cultures that live along the equator, such as parts of Africa, Central America, and the South Pacific, are sometimes characterized as slow and unfocused. It's difficult to overcome the malaise which oppresses curiosity and inventiveness.

On November 13, 1943, an odd feeling of electrical current permeated the atmosphere. Throughout the afternoon, after I gave up trying to sleep in the beach house after a long shift, I watched dark purple clouds gather on the southeast horizon. Everyone slinked along the paths between the shacks in slow motion and silent, as if to not disturb the sky gods. By that evening, a fearsome gale careened through the camp. Before midnight moaning bands of drenching rain blew roofs off the shacks and destroyed foods that individuals had so painstakingly hoarded. This happened before the typhoon fully made landfall.

All staff and volunteers were called to move as many patients as possible from the open air wards and shacks, into brick or stone buildings. At daylight the dreaded typhoon hit Manila like a bull's eye was painted on the cathedral dome. Huge roofs hurtled through the air, whole cars tumbled along the roads, and all within the walls of Santo Tomas was quickly flooded. For three hours nurses hovered over patients who weren't even awake to fear for their own lives. Once the storm passed, the job of clearing the destruction began. Within a day bloated animal bodies fouled the air. A self-appointed committee took over hauling those corpses away, occasionally turning up a human body. It was too dangerous for everyone to start wading around, since snakes were a considerable threat. The flooded lower floors of buildings were evacuated, and everyone moved upstairs. Sewer lines weren't functional and outdoor privies were destroyed, so we reverted to using buckets. The crowding, heat, and stench turned Santo Tomas into a hellish compound, which could have been relieved somewhat by releasing the civilian women. The Japanese would have nothing to do with that idea. All they did was transfer about one hundred men to another prison.

The typhoon destroyed most of the gardens that we internees had so carefully tended, and the absence of those fresh vegetables was immediately felt. For over two weeks, our captors served only a thin gruel, often including worms and insect parts. When your body is visibly wasting away, you will eat anything. I often thought about all the food wasted from the elegant dinners served when we first arrived at Sternberg.

Mona said, "Just shut your eyes, hold your nose, and pretend its Granny Ellen's raisin pudding!"

The four of us were determined to survive the war, but we admitted there was a limit to how long each of us could hold on. With so much damage over the whole area, even the locals had little extra food to sell.

Miraculously, the commandant allowed parcels from the Red Cross to be delivered in December. Each internee received a box which held soap, Spam, powdered milk, jam, tinned butter, cigarettes, and an article of clothing. One might think that it wasn't enough food to make a difference, but I have to say it was enough to keep us alive a little longer. In a few weeks the local vendors began offering food-stuffs imported from islands that had not been damaged so heavily by the typhoon. Their prices were inflated, but we carefully spent our hoarded money on dried meats and fresh fruit. Our physical appearances didn't change, but we all felt so much better. We thought Mabel was suffering with scurvy, and after a few meals that included citrus fruit, the symptoms subsided.

While we each had the chore of finding and hording food for ourselves, the hospital shifts still demanded our time and energy. We never got around to every patient on the shifts, because it took two nurses to treat each one. Turning and lifting the men and women who couldn't do for themselves was too hard for one nurse in our weakened condition. Those patients were so brave, enduring our feeble attempts to make them comfortable. From their lips, we'd often hear, "You're an angel!" The elderly nuns, who had been a miraculous force in the wards, no longer had the strength to work. They tried to help by rinsing out bloody bandages; however, hauling and heating the water finally proved to be too much.

In mid-January, 1944, an announcement was made to the effect that Santo Tomas was no longer an internment camp. The commandant issued an order that all those inside the walls were prisoners of war. Immediately we saw the changes: rations were drastically cut, and by February package days were stopped. Guards could be bribed to sneak bags of food into camp, that is, if you had the cash. Adults agreed to cut their rations even more, so that children would receive the same amount as usual. My heart broke watching mothers deny their hunger, in order to feed a son or daughter the starvation rations provided. As the camp ran out of sugar, salt, and oil, terrible new maladies began appearing. The doctors were finally able to persuade the commandant to restore scant supplies of salt to prevent the crippling results from having none.

Our guards dealt out more beatings after the internees' status changed to prisoners of war. I believe that they felt pressured by rumors of the Allies gaining ground, so tempers were short. We were quick to bow and show respect, but many civilians in Santo Tomas felt at least a cuff on the head or jab in the back. Occasionally, we were forced to witness a particularly harsh punishment, which made us wonder who would be next.

As the spring approached, Mona spent her resting time away from our rebuilt shack. One evening she confided that Dr. Chester Carlisle, or Chet, had stolen her heart.

"Can you believe it? I am a POW, in love with another POW; clearly against my rules!" she laughed. But she was so happy in the middle of a horrible place. I had to agree that Chet Carlisle suited Mona in every way. He cared so much about the suffering of others, especially children. Chet began dropping by our beach house occasionally, to talk about something besides surgeries. When I saw him and Mona together, hanging on each word the other said, I felt the absence of my own love…my husband, Lee. My husband! I wanted to know about him. Where was he, and was he alright? I could have lost my mind wanting to touch his face and feel his arms around me in the night.

"Remember when I told you what Ma said about crossroads we come to in our lives?" I said to Mona one late night, as we monitored two patients recovering from surgery. The skies were dark, with a rumble of thunder in the distance, but the wards were quiet. Mona had a cigarette that we passed back and forth in the dim corner.

"Yes. Your Ma is a wise person, Ivy."

"I keep thinking that this hell-hole is a crossroads of sorts. I've got to stay sane and alive, because there will be life beyond this barricade for us all. People I love expect me to somehow get to the next intersection, so I will!" And then I cried, because I couldn't make Lee's face clear in my mind. Later, I took our marriage certificate from its hiding place, and read every word over and over.

Several Army nurses had fallen in love with soldiers when we were still in Bataan and Corregidor; like me, they suffered with the knowledge the men were being held in a prison or work camp, or had died. We seldom spoke among ourselves about our soldiers, but agreed that if they were kept together, perhaps their spirits were not broken. Unspoken between us was the certainty that their captivity was cruel and inhumane.

When Lydia's ring money was spent, I unfastened another silver charm from the bracelet to buy more dried meat. The guards could still be bribed, so we dealt with vendors through them. The guards whispered that it was from monkeys or wild pigs. My friends just called our provisions "mystery meat," and ate it without any questions. I never thought I'd miss having my menstrual period, but most of us hadn't had one for a year. In one way it was good to not have to fool with it, but the lack of a period was another sign our bodies were failing.

Our unit of the Army Nurse Corps was seldom together at the same time. Captain Roberts called a meeting one Sunday morning in May, 1944, under the guise of a religious service. It was shocking to see so many of us in such deplorable condition gathered in one place. Many nurses were bent over like eighty year old women, hobbling on crippled feet, with knobby knees and elbows prominently showing above stick-like long bones. Captain Roberts was so thin that she wore rope suspenders to keep her slacks from sliding down her hips. She looked around the room, and made certain there were no English speaking guards nearby.

"Quickly I'll just say that news is coming in that the allies are nearing the Philippines, and it seems as if our enemy is losing ground. I am so proud of my nurses. Yes, you are *my* nurses" she said, with a catch in her throat. "Your professional efforts and dignity will certainly see us through until liberation. It is my dream to see you all standing on U.S. soil again." We burst into applause, which caused the guards to scream and force us out of the room.

A few representatives from the Red Cross were allowed inside the walls of Santo Tomas in late June; however, they were permitted to dispense only small quantities of vitamins and quinine. One of the women wound her way along the narrow paths between hundreds of cots and pallets, taking the time to speak to some of the most ill. The young matron took a photo of Mona and I when the guards weren't watching. A few years later I acquired a copy of that photo, and included the following comment when I pasted it into Ma's photo album:

*"By July of '44 my hair began falling out; malnutrition was our meanest enemy. I was never so hungry, even back in the hard days on the ranch. All of us looked angular, with jutting shoulder blades and bony hips. I sold another silver charm from my bracelet to buy some rice, dried mystery meat, and a few bananas, since the daily ration had been reduced again to about 700 calories. Chewing on a strip of dried meat, one of my teeth just fell out. My gums were so swollen that all my teeth were loose, so I had to be more careful after that. Mabel was no longer able to work, which meant she received less food. I was afraid that was the fate of us all. Our misery was compounded by the downpours that came every afternoon, turning the shacks into steaming boxes that the resident rats invaded to escape the torrents rushing down the paths. Every night, I wondered if I would*

*ever see my lover again. My life in Fort Rock was just a faint memory."*

Two prisoners, British men who worked for an oil company before the invasion, were captured after their short-lived escape over the wall one night. No amount of pleading by their friends swayed the commandant, who ordered the men shot the next morning. Everyone in the camp was ordered to witness the execution, and the commandant's rambling speech warned us that the men's deaths would serve as an example to others planning an escape. There had been other escapes when men's bodies were still healthy, and money was plentiful enough to bribe guards. It was rumored that about twenty prisoners got away during the typhoon the previous fall. I steeled myself for the execution, but nothing prepares a person, even a nurse, for what happens when a bullet penetrates the skull. I told myself that the men were lucky to have a quick death, instead of slow torture to the same result.

A smuggled note from Lydia's friends informed us that they had arranged to leave Manila because it was rumored that U.S. bombing would begin soon. They had not been allowed to send us food for a long time, but we could never repay them for the help we received early in our internment.

Rations were cut again and again to the point where the amount of rice allotted to each prisoner was a few tablespoons. We were lucky if some flakes of fish or coconut were stirred into the ration. The camp's death rate had held steady at two or three a month until the summer of 1944, when we began to lose that many each week. Patients were exhausted trying to fight off infections with starving bodies. The cases of beriberi, pellagra, and scurvy skyrocketed, and we begged for more nutritious food to replace the deficiencies. There was no protective fat left on anyone, so internal organs were prone to injury from simple bumps. We tried to grow vegetables once more, but other starving prisoners pulled up the plants just for the tiny green stems. I wasn't angry, just disappointed.

Mona told me that Chet could no longer perform surgeries, since he hadn't the strength to stand for long periods, and his hands shook terribly. I couldn't bear to see him melting into a shadow of himself. My last silver charm, the two hearts linked with the diamond, was traded for mystery meat, flat bread loaves, butter, onions, bananas and a bottle of wine. The four of us plus Chet gathered at the shack to eat just half of the food; we spread the remainder over the next three days. We drank the wine like a cordial, sipping just a little after each meal. Chet and Mona announced with great fanfare that they would marry after we returned home. We toasted their happiness and I prayed we all would last that long.

Towards the end of September we heard bombing and saw smoke coming from the Manila port area. American planes flew over the camp, which sent the prisoners into spasms of revelry! Those who could stand up tried to dance, but most were too fragile to do anything but clap and sing. Everyone thought that the camp would be liberated in a matter of days, but that proved to be wrong. The Japanese might be losing the war, but they weren't about to ease our suffering.

Radio reports that passed through the camp disclosed that U.S. troops had advanced against the Japanese, hoping to take the Philippines by November. But that didn't happen, so we waited and watched more Santo Tomas prisoners die. Most of the nurses attempted to help patients as best they could, but in reality we were in the same condition as the ones we treated.

October, November, and December passed, while we subsisted on one meal of rice a day. I had already traded my bracelet chain for food and we had nothing else to offer. In January a report circulated which said the Americans had taken Luzon, and were marching towards Manila. Allied bombers flew sorties over the city every day, dropping bombs on Japanese installations and ships in the harbor. We waited, and starved. My bones felt as brittle as dry corn stalks, and my gait was stiff, with scant flexing of my ankles. I told Mona that all I needed was a squirt from the grease gun we used on the old pickup at home. In spite of her own pain, she giggled madly.

Early in January, one of the doctors quietly told me that there was a break in the back fence which was being used by some internees at night to bring food into the camp. We had no money, but something had to be done to keep us from starving before the Americans came. Mona and I argued over which of us would go, but I drew the long straw. I waited a couple of nights until the cover of rain and wind in the darkness gave me an added advantage. Once I found the opening, I rolled under the fence and kept rolling across a wide field of grass until I bumped into a concrete block building. I lay very still for what seemed an eternity. Finally, hunched low, I worked my way along the rear walls of small shops until I smelled fresh bread. When I peeped through a small window, I saw a baker taking flat bread loaves from the huge oven. He spread them out to cool on large racks, and then turned off the lamps. When he left through the front door, I looked for a way to break into the building.

Relief washed over my body when the door gave way with a hard push. It took just two or three minutes to gather several loaves into a towel, which I knotted and slung over my shoulder. When I was only a few yards from the building on my way back, a hand grabbed my shoulder. Stifling a scream, I spun around, and was face to face with the baker. He thrust a bowl of butter into my hands, and then disappeared into the darkness. The rain had slacked, and I took my time crawling back across the field to the fence, where Mona anxiously stood watch for my return. By rationing the bread and butter, we made it last ten days. I believe it saved our lives, and I never forgot the kindness of that Filipino baker.

On February 2, 1945, we awoke to an absence of guards on the grounds, and someone reported that the commandant's headquarters were vacant. The Japanese left no food and we were too weak to leave the camp.

The next day tanks rumbled through the main gate of Santo Tomas! When American soldiers walked into the hospital ward, I tried to run meet them, but stumbled and fell onto my knees. Before I could push up on my feet, a smiling G.I. tenderly lifted me into his arms. He was the first healthy person I'd seen in a long time, and I was overwhelmed by his strength.

# CHAPTER 19

OUR LIBERATORS, THE AMERICAN 44TH TANK BATTALION embraced us with honor and appreciation. They picked up on our nickname "Angels of Bataan," given by the men and women under our care through the years. I felt humbled by all the attention and we soon heard that our imprisonment story was already in the newspapers back home. I cannot begin to describe what a long, hot shower with real shampoo felt like. Most of us had patches of impetigo on our faces and scalps. We were a sorry looking bunch but were treated like queens. Within a day, each of us was provided two new uniforms, and the feel of that clean cloth on my skin brought tears to my eyes. Mona smoothed the skirt over her emaciated hips, and still managed to look snappy. Chet Carlisle assured Mona he'd join her in the U.S. in a few months. Although he was frail and needed time to recuperate, Chet left Santo Tomas to reunite with other civilian doctors to treat the citizens of Manila caught in the cross-fire.

Lydia located her friends who had returned to the city, and they persuaded her to move in with them until she returned to the U.S. We had shared too much history to stray far from each other's thoughts, and agreed to meet back home in the next few months. Mabel's health had deteriorated the last month to a dangerous level, so she was transported to a hospital unit that was leaving immediately for a U.S. base. Some other nurses, including Captain Roberts, would be on the same flight, hurrying them to the best care available. The rest of us were flown to Leyte, away from the burning city of Manila.

Right away we were encouraged to write our families, although they had already been notified by the Army that Santo Tomas was liberated. I wished that I could see Ma's and Lizzy's faces when they read my letter. It was difficult to believe my ordeal was actually over. No one in Manila had any information about the soldiers who were taken when Bataan fell. I still had hope that Lee was alive because I couldn't imagine a future without him. If he had indeed been taken to Japan, I knew it could be months before he would be freed, since Japan was still fighting to the end. My goal until then was regaining my health.

Food! Lots of food! Hamburgers, fried potatoes, tomatoes, and milk were my dream foods; I only had to ask and it was served! Fried chicken, biscuits, and gravy, which tasted almost as good as Ma's, was on the menu next. I gained several pounds within a short time and my skin quickly looked healthier. I fretted about my thin hair, worried that it would not ever grow back as thick as it was.

It felt like we nurses were a top priority for the Army, in the way the officials organized our transport back home. Two weeks after liberation, our journey hop-scotched across the Pacific and stopped in Hawaii for a rest on the island's sunny beaches. The Army advanced some of our back pay, which we used to buy make up, underwear, perfumes, and many silly items. Oh, it felt so good to have silky fabric against my skin after the years of wearing coarse, tattered clothing. When the plane set down in San Francisco on February 23, 1945, a crowd had gathered at the side of the tarmac. As we deplaned, faces in the crowd became clearer and I ran towards my own Ma! Granny Ellen was there too, and the three of us rocked back and forth, kissing and hugging.

"Oh, my girl, you're just a bag of bones! What did they do to you?" Ma cried.

"We were so worried all the time, Ivy!" Granny cried. "I was afraid I wouldn't ever see you again!"

Mona's oldest sister came to meet her, with the sad news of their mother's death just a few months earlier. Many of the nurses heard similar reports about relatives, which made the reunion bittersweet.

Soon the nurses were scooped up, along with families, and transported to the Army hospital, where we spent a week being evaluated and treated. Ma and Granny stayed with me during the days, and we tried to catch up on all that had happened at home since we last saw each other. All the nurses slept a lot during that time, finally released from worry and fear. True to form, Ma and Granny enveloped Mona with their love, and spent many hours visiting with her. I was embarrassed when Ma noticed that I had food hidden among my belongings, but she said Mona was doing the same thing. Irrational as it sounds, I guess we were worried that all the food in the dining room might disappear. It took years before I got over that obsession.

The Army had cautioned the families about asking for too many details of our time in Santo Tomas Internment Camp, so Ma and Granny avoided prodding me about that. In time, in small increments, I shared most of my story over coffee at Ma's kitchen table in Fort Rock. Before leaving San Francisco, a motherly lieutenant assigned to facilitate our return to the U.S., took us on a shopping spree. All I owned up to that point were two uniforms which weren't a very good fit and the few items I bought in Hawaii. I couldn't wait to get into Levi's and a plaid shirt, or a stylish dress with shoes to match.

Newspapers across the country carried the story of our liberation and arrival back on U.S. soil. In many cases the reporters omitted the truths and wrote what their readers would pay money to read. Some articles said that the nurses had "suffered unimaginable atrocities, including rape, at the hands of their Japanese captors." The Army quickly quelled any hint of this, because every one of the nurses had been asked by the doctors, and denied such abuse. All of us became tired of the sensationalism, and just looked forward to our sixty-day leave. For me, this meant traveling by train with Ma and Granny to Eugene, where Lizzy, Uncle Bob and Amy welcomed me back.

Seeing everyone was wonderful, and I felt obligated to let them understand that I was okay. Lizzy was all grown up, and a junior at the university, living with Granny like I did. She promised to come home during their spring break in late March. The next day Ma and I took the bus to Bend.

By the time we reached Bend my stamina had evaporated. Mr. Atkins met us at the bus station, where Ma introduced me to her husband! Everyone kept the secret so well and I hadn't noticed that Ma was wearing a wedding band. She was pleased with herself, surprising me with her news, and Allen Atkins looked upon his bride with loving eyes.

Lee's parents were also at the station in Bend, and we visited over coffee before leaving. They knew Lee and I had married on Bataan. I assumed they learned from Ma, but they showed me a card Lee wrote after the surrender in Bataan. The Red Cross gathered post cards from some soldiers before they were marched north to imprisonment, and managed to get those to the U.S. As I read Lee's words on the worn card, I felt his presence warm my heart.

"Mom and Pop, General Wainwright surrendered and we are being sent to prison camps. I am okay. Ivy and I are married. I pray she gets safely home soon. I love you both, Lee."

"We haven't heard a word since, Ivy. But when the war is over, we'll all be together again!" Lee's mom remarked in a shrill voice.

We all were aware how slim his chances were to survive the years of punishing labor he was surely forced to do. I hugged Mrs. Johnson, and confirmed that we'd soon have a big reunion.

The Bend Bulletin newspaper sent a reporter to get a photo of my return, and asked for a statement. All I could say was "I'm so glad to be home."

I was overwhelmed and turned to Ma, saying, "Take me home, please." Ma told the Johnsons to come see us at the ranch in a week or two, and I could only hope the war would be over by then.

I stretched out in the back seat of Mr. Atkins' car, rolled down the window, and pushed all bad thoughts from my mind. Listening to Ma and her husband banter back and forth, I knew Mr. Atkins was perfect in every way for Ma and spoiled her no end. We drove home in his comfortable International Station Wagon, over a much improved road leading to Fort Rock.

The closer we got to Fort Rock, the more I worried that it might have changed too much. I wanted everything the same, for a short time, anyway. However, when we turned through the gate, and I saw the differences, it was alright. Sunny, our old hound, bounded up to the car when I opened the door, and licked my face when I bent to hug him.

"Oh, Sunny, I missed you so much! We'll take a long walk this evening, I promise!" I cried. He begged to have his ears scratched, and sat still with his tongue hanging out the side of his jaw while I obliged him. He hadn't changed a bit, and I told him so.

The old ranch house had a new roof, windows, and a coat of paint. The inside was completely renovated with a butane refrigerator and cooking range, new furniture and flooring. Tom's room had been enlarged to hold two twin beds. My old sleeping alcove was incorporated to enlarge the parlor. I turned to Ma in amazement, and she proudly said the work was a wedding present from Mr. Atkins…Allen.

"We split our time between here and Allen's Lakeview apartment over the store," she said, smiling in his direction. "You know, I really like helping in the store, something I never thought I'd say."

I bumped her shoulder with mine, and replied, "I can tell you are really happy, Ma. He seems like a very nice man. I'm just sorry I wasn't here for the wedding."

"To be honest, I felt guilty going ahead without you. We just went before Judge Clinton, with Allen's son and Lizzy standing up with us two years ago this October."

I squeezed her hands, saying, "We each missed the other's weddings, Ma, but that's okay."

Anxious to move to another subject, Ma bustled around, helping me unpack. Allen came inside after checking on the barnyard animals, and brought their ranch hand in to meet me.

"When Red enlisted, his little brother, Harry, offered to take care of things when we are gone," Allen said, clapping his hand on Harry's shoulder. We all laughed at the "little brother" remark, since the young man was over six feet tall. Allen continued, "Harry is a great hand, moving the cattle around…oh, Ivy, we forgot to tell you we bought a couple of horses. Harry has the little mare broken to the saddle, but you'll get to train her like you want."

"I've got to go see her! Come on, Sunny, let's check her out!" I darted out of the house, just as excited as a kid at Christmas.

Allen was anxious to return to the store in Lakeview, although it appeared he left it in the capable hands of a long-time employee. When he and Ma left for a few days, I welcomed the solitude, interrupted only by Harry's coming and going. I'm sure Ma realized that I craved some time alone after all the excitement of coming home.

Our cow, Brownie, had been given to a young family who could use the milk and butter. Ma said that with all of us gone it didn't make sense to keep her. The rhubarb plant was still going strong by the kitchen door, and Ma promised on her next visit she'd bake a pie. A few chickens pecked around the yard. I reminded myself to lock them in the coop when the sun went down, to keep a coyote from snagging a meal. I felt an incredible pleasure at making little decisions, instead of life and death matters.

I spent most of the next week on the little mare's back. She was called Rusty, was five years old, and had a saucy attitude. At first I could ride only a few minutes, but soon my stamina improved and I slowly increased our range. The two of us soon roamed the buttes and valleys far from home, with Sunny loping along beside us. I'd pack a lunch and a canvas bag of water at sunrise, and the three of us would spend four or five hours away from the house. One day we explored around the town's namesake, the rock "fort," which was every bit as big as I remembered. Lee came to mind so many times, since the two of us grew up playing cowboys and Indians around its base. I wondered if we would ever eat lunch in its shadow again.

The war raged on, in both the Pacific and Europe, but General Eisenhower and the President assured all of us on the home front that our boys would be coming home soon. My brother Tom was at a base in England, and Ma wouldn't be happy until he was safe under her roof. He wrote me a long letter about his last three years, and how worried he was that I might not come back. Tom knew about my marriage, and that Lee was a POW. He was positive that Lee could survive most anything, and I loved my big brother for saying that. Tom knew about Ma and Allen's marriage, and was genuinely happy for them.

On one of Ma's trips back to the ranch, she brought a copy of the Bend Bulletin, showing a photo of us on the front page. The headline read, "Our Angel of Bataan Glad to Be Home." The article below the photo just repeated the press release from the Army which I had already read.

When I'd been home almost three weeks, friends started dropping in, and by that time I was ready to see them. Edith came, showing off her little boy, and pulled out a photo of her husband in his navy uniform. Ma already told me that he had been killed when his ship was torpedoed in the Mediterranean Sea. I thought, "She's too young to be a widow," and then realized how many women lost loved ones in that same sinking. We watched her son chase the chickens, and he squealed with excitement when I sat him on Rusty's back. I was sure that Edith would find a daddy to help raise her son. Her visit only magnified how much I wanted to have a baby with Lee.

Ma's old pickup jostled me all the way to Silver Lake, and I visited a few days with Aunt Fay. The sweet thing hadn't wanted to bother me just yet, but I found myself craving her insights and opinions on some decisions I would soon make. Fay's son and wife moved to Portland a few months after the war started, after he was rejected by all the military branches due to a heart murmur. Fay, like Papa, had lived in the valley all her life, and although she had many friends nearby, she was lonesome. Her son begged her to move closer, and I knew she would eventually go.

One evening when Ma was at the ranch, I asked her what happened with my other brother, Michael's, wife and baby.

"I never saw anything of her, or the money I sent," she said. "She saw a chance to take advantage of my sorrow, so I was easily tricked. I doubt there was any marriage or baby, but we'll never know. I hate that I couldn't bury Michael here on the ranch, but the oil rig was offshore, and collapsed. His body was never found."

"Why don't we build a bench down by the spring where he liked to hang out?" I suggested. "We'll carve his name on it, and think of all the good things that Michael did."

"He wasn't all bad, you know," Ma affirmed. "He followed Papa around the ranch and would do anything for him. It seemed like after your Papa died, Michael was lost."

"Like I said, we'll just remember all the good things, Ma."

Lizzy's spring break at home was like the sun shined every day for me. Her energy and optimism were contagious and soon she had Ma, Allen, and I ditching chores to chase rainbows instead. We drove to several ice caves one day and spent a couple of hours at a hot spring sauna another afternoon. When Ma and Allen returned to Lakeview, Lizzy and I explored a canyon near Klamath Falls to see the petroglyphs left by Native Americans on rock walls. In the evenings we'd lie in bed and talk about her plans after graduation and what was going to happen to the ranch. Tom's letters had convinced our Ma that he wasn't going to take over the ranch when the war ended, and Lizzy wanted to stay in Eugene and teach school. Although Ma and Allen could take care of the ranch with their part time arrangement right then, later it would be too much to handle. I had a lot to think about and told myself that my future depended on Lee.

I selfishly dreaded Lizzy's return to Eugene, but she said she would come home again later in the summer. When Ma was at the ranch, she cooked big meals, and I made her very happy by eating more than my share.

Before we had to report back to the hospital in San Francisco, Mona wrote asking if she could come to the ranch. It was a remarkable reunion for the two of us; like me, she had put on weight and her skin and hair looked healthier. We both desperately needed the dental work promised to everyone, since the years of malnutrition had taken a toll on us all.

Mona told me that her family never quit asking questions about her internment, wanting all the details. She tried to explain to them why it was hard to talk about, but no one listened, not even her sister. In desperation, Mona took a bus to Boise and got a room in a tourist cabin and finally wrote to me.

"They didn't believe that I could be imprisoned for so long and escape being raped. I got tired of the looks and whispers," Mona admitted.

"Why didn't you come here right away? This is your home, Mona, whenever you want. After all we've been through you should know that you don't have to ask." Our days were filled with chores, reading, and cooking. We talked half the nights away and wondered how the other "angels" were doing back home. Mona was so hilarious around our white-face cattle. The first time I made her accompany me on foot into the pasture near the house, she was petrified. We'd load the pickup with hay bales every morning, and drive out on the range. She would cut the bale string and toss the hay out while I slowly drove through the herd. With the last bale, we'd stop to watch the calves nosing up to their mamas, and walk among the cattle to check for infections or other problems. Mona soon learned to push through the firmly planted animals, and watch out for her feet. Ma arrived that weekend with a bucket of big syringes to inoculate our herd. Mona learned how to get an animal securely immobilized in Grandpa's old cattle chute. More than once she got butted to the ground, but no injuries resulted.

She just giggled, "I'll sure have stories to tell my grandkids!" We looked at each other, and then fell into a paroxysm of laughter. Ma even caught our reason for humor: in the last few years we had already accumulated a lifetime of stories to tell.

Mona had a letter from Chet before she left Idaho, promising to be back in the states by August. She was so in love, desperately in love, never dreaming that she could feel so deeply for anyone. Theirs was a simple love, no surprises or secrets; my love for Lee had been complicated and convoluted, but nevertheless, it was complete. Mona and I were simply going through the motions of living, until our men were home.

# CHAPTER 20

A FEW DAYS AFTER WE ARRIVED IN San Francisco, Germany surrendered. The war in Europe was over when Hitler committed suicide a few days earlier. A wild celebration on the streets erupted and I was actually happy we were in a big city to be crazy with thousands of other revelers! On the first night after surrender, Mona, Mabel, and I drank too many beers with two Army doctors, and were in no shape to be interviewed by the psychiatrist the next day. It was actually very funny, and no one reprimanded us for the infraction.

The doctors already knew enough about returning POWs to expect cases of "flashbacks." Most of us admitted we suffered from nightmares; my biggest concern was how all that affected my family. While I was home Ma and Lizzy helped me through more than a few bad nights, and I realized that Mona was as scarred as I was.

Physically, I was returning to normal, and began having my monthly period. With the great foods I'd been fed at home, my gums had begun to heal, so the Army dentists began their work, replacing my rotten teeth. Some of the nurses, who were in such poor shape when we were liberated, weren't released from the hospital to return home on leave like most of us. Their treatment and recovery was a slow road, and several suffered life-long ailments related to their ordeal in Santo Tomas. Luckily, Mabel improved quickly and had just returned from a month's leave with her parents. It was a relief when we saw how healthy she looked, since she had suffered from more illnesses than Mona or me.

Sometimes it seemed like the time in Santo Tomas happened to someone else, not me. I felt like an observer, instead of a survivor. I guess it was my way of dealing with things that were too awful to accept. The images of burned flesh and diseased bodies haunted me almost every day, so no wonder I chose to believe the nurse at Santo Tomas was someone I didn't know.

The city celebrated the whole time we were there, which was understandable. Most of us nurses who were well enough went dancing two or three times a week. Neither Mona nor I were looking for boyfriends but there were plenty of soldiers who just wanted to hold a girl and enjoy the evening at a crowded ballroom.

We also went to the movie theater often, and especially loved *Going My Way* and *Meet Me in St. Louis*. The newsreels were hard to watch, since most showed hills covered with dead Japanese soldiers, as they continued to fight an already lost war. I wanted to scream, "Surrender!" so Lee could come home. Hadn't we given enough?

Right before July 4th, 1945, Mona and I resigned our commissions, and were released from the hospital. Trains were packed with soldiers who had just returned from Europe, so we bought bus tickets and sat on our suitcases all the way to Eugene. Granny and Lizzy hadn't expected us, but within a few minutes two bedrooms were ready. I wanted nothing but to roll up in a quilt and sleep for a week. Ma and Allen drove up two days later, with news that Tom would be home on leave within three weeks. Ma and Granny talked about several families they knew who lost sons and husbands; suddenly they realized how painful it must be for me to listen, not knowing if I was one of those widows.

Mona and I returned to the ranch with a lust for hard work,

wanting to be so exhausted at the end of the day that we'd fall into bed right after supper. Ma's young farm hand helped us rebuild the old corral, bigger and better. The barn was built to last by my Grandpa, but we decided to add two stalls and then painted the weathered gray siding red. Each day our routine was to be up with the sunrise, drink coffee on the porch, and plan our day. Ma usually arrived on Saturday evening and stayed until Monday afternoon. On those days she'd make a big "stick to your ribs" breakfast. The hard work did help me get through the days of waiting for the Japanese to surrender; however, at night Mona knew my pain. She received a letter from Chet, asking her to meet him in San Diego on August 25th. I was truly happy for them, but ached for news of Lee.

Mona proposed a suggestion to me. She and Chet wanted me to follow them to California to continue my nursing career. The idea was tempting because she and I understood each other, what we'd been through. I loved Mona for thinking about my future, but I still had my money on Lee's return.

Tom arrived home a week earlier than expected, on a Sunday afternoon with Lizzy, which almost put Ma in a faint. Tom danced Ma around the room, and teased her about being a new bride. Allen drove up the next day, so we had a long awaited family reunion. Tom took me aside in the evening to talk about the ranch. All of us wanted it to stay in the family for now, but I couldn't make any promises on my part just yet. He remarked how good the ranch looked, and the anticipated success with a good breeding program. I went to bed with a lot on my mind, and tossed all night.

About five o'clock the next morning, I pulled on my Levi's and work shirt, and watched the sunrise. The meadowlarks were singing, cattle were lowing in the pasture, and I could hear my horse, Rusty, stomping in her stall. The bitter smell of sagebrush drifted in from the hills and mixed with the sweetness of alfalfa. A red-tailed hawk soared across the yard looking for mice, and ascended abruptly to perch on the old windmill. Sunny crawled out from under the porch to sprawl at my feet, secure in his role on the ranch. He and I finally walked to the barn and opened Rusty's stall so she could prance around the corral.

Tom appeared at my side, and tossed some hay to the horses.

"As much as I don't want to be a rancher, it sure smells good around here," he said.

"Ranching is a headache, you know, and a person would be crazy to take it on if they had a chance to do something else," I replied. "I do have a nursing career that I love." And Tom nodded as he worked.

We worked in silence for a few minutes, and could smell the coffee brewing in the kitchen, so Ma was up.

"Tom…I've decided I'm going to do it…take over the ranch, I mean," I stammered.

"What about the nursing? I don't want you to sacrifice something you love."

"Who says I can't do both? I'll figure it out!" I smiled. "For so long I was convinced that I couldn't make this decision until Lee came home, but I've realized that the ranch means so much to me that I want to be here even if Lee doesn't make it back." When he squeezed my shoulders under his arm, and nodded that he understood, an involuntary sob escaped my throat. But quickly I caught myself.

"I'm okay, really." I rubbed the horses' noses, comforted by the big animals' trust.

Tom asked, "Can I be a cowboy once in awhile?"

"Come anytime!" I laughed. "We'll have to sit down and figure out how I can buy each of your shares of the ranch and livestock. I want to make it right with you and Lizzy."

"I'll bet you a hundred dollars that Ma already has that worked out!"

he said. "Are you ready to tell her?" I took a deep breath and nodded.

Tom was right; Ma was a step ahead of me. Her notebook contained a list of all inventory on the ranch, including livestock and equipment. She had worked out a fair payment I owed to my brother and sister.

"Ma, you should be included and paid something; after all, the ranch wouldn't be the success it is today without your hard work," I insisted.

"Allen and I have talked this over. The ranch belongs to you children, but I might want to rustle a beef off the ranch once in awhile!" Ma said.

Tom suggested we set up a ten-year payment schedule, and Lizzy agreed. Ma interrupted with the news that she hadn't used our Army allotments for over two years. With that money I could pay Lizzy and Tom cash up front for part of my indebtedness, and save back several hundred dollars to cover expenses until some cattle were sold. Satisfied that the ranch's future was settled at last, Ma declared that she was going to bake a rhubarb pie, and disappeared into the kitchen.

"I'll be spending some of my cash on an engagement ring," Tom proudly announced, grinning from ear to ear. "Ma and Lizzy have known about Ruth for a year. I met her in England, and want to bring her to the U.S. so we can get married." He flipped out his wallet to show me a photo of Ruth, a dark-haired beauty.

"Why hadn't you told me already? I think that's wonderful!" I said, pecking him on the cheek. "What are you going to do now, stay in the Army?"

"No, I'm getting out and want a job with one of the big airplane manufacturers, maybe like Boeing in Seattle."

Seeing my family so happy, I made a conscious effort to keep the conversation from drifting to Lee. Everyone would become depressed and feel guilty for enjoying life, and also worry more about me if we discussed the question of Lee's return.

The attorney in Lakeview took care of the legal end of our agreement about the ranch, and then Tom and Mona left together. He reported to a base in Portland where he processed out of the Army, and Mona traveled by train to San Diego. Chet wrote enthusiastically about a position in a Los Angeles hospital. Mona made me promise that after they got settled I'd come visit, but it was years before I made that trip. She was always close to my heart, and not a week went by without a letter going one way or the other. Lizzy returned to Eugene, and my ranch hand decided to move to Klamath Falls. I was finally alone, but being on the ranch brought comfort, every day, every night.

The headlines on August 6th were shocking: a U.S. plane dropped an atomic bomb on Hiroshima, Japan! Another Japanese city was struck, followed a week later by Japan's surrender. We were at peace at last!

# CHAPTER 21

DAYS DRAGGED INTO WEEKS, WITH NO WORD about Lee until September 25th, when I received an official looking envelope from the Army. My hands trembled so violently that I wasn't sure I could even get it open. Tempted at first to drive to Lakeview before reading the letter, I settled on a glass of whiskey from the bottle Tom left behind, and sat on the porch steps. With Sunny leaning against my knee, I slid my fingernail under the flap of the envelope, and slowly brought the folded pages out. Before reading the message, I told myself that I was ready for any news of Lee, but I really wasn't.

It was addressed to "Mrs. Lee Johnson, Reese Ranch Fort Rock, Oregon." While I was in San Francisco, I used our certificate of marriage to prove I was married to Lee. The Army accepted the forms that updated his information, and insured that I'd be informed when they knew something about him. The letter was from an officer in charge of prisoners of war who had just been liberated from Japanese work camps. Survivors from Lee's company, who were also sent to Japan, reported that Lee was seen still alive in June, working in a mine near the town of Omuda. However, when the camp was liberated, he wasn't there. The other prisoners said he disappeared one night. There was no record of his being executed, like so many others, but the only other explanation was that he escaped. While the Army said that he could still be alive somewhere in Japan, I could read between the lines of their notification. Having been held in a POW camp myself, I knew that escape was difficult and dangerous; but I still held out hope.

I wasn't sure if the Johnsons were notified, so I sent a letter to them right away. I could only imagine the pain they suffered at the thought of losing their only child. For some reason, I decided to wait a couple of weeks before telling Ma, as if I might receive another letter with better news. Eventually, one evening in October I drove to Lakeview, and told Ma and Allen. When I said the words aloud, I had to admit that if Lee were alive, he would've been found by now. I cried that night in Ma's arms, my heart broken.

The ranch saved my sanity that fall, with preparations for winter, baling hay and moving it under cover, and looking for a bull to add to the breeding pool. The herd was still small enough for me to move it around the ranch, but I'd have to hire help before the spring calves were born. I'd been reading up on herd improvement, producing more meat on the hoof and preventing diseases common on ranches in Oregon and California.

I'd worried that I might not want to be a nurse after the horrible experience of war. But when the school principal in Silver Lake asked if I could work two days a week doing vision and hearing tests on the students, I was so excited! It was an easy assignment, and the children made it so interesting. I looked forward to those days, but the job only lasted a month. Ma said if I was interested, she'd heard that the Lakeview clinic could use another nurse a few days a week. Although I wasn't ready to commute so far from the ranch, it was something I might consider in a few months. I made a point of subscribing to nursing journals to keep up with new techniques.

Lydia wrote that she was back in California with her sons, adjusting to life in the "land of plenty." All the gals in our foursome were thankful for the little things we had, after the years of deprivation.

I finally gained enough weight that I could wear the ring Ma gave me for high school graduation, without it slipping off my finger. She noticed and beamed with pride. I marked it as one more hurdle jumped on my way to normalcy.

My life fell into a comfortable routine of ranch chores, riding Rusty, and even learning new recipes to surprise Ma and Allen when they'd come for dinner. Allen helped me build the bench for Michael that we'd discussed, and it turned out just as I had envisioned. I carved Michael's name into the seat back, then we carried it in the wagon to the spring. Ma sat on it the first evening, and insisted that she felt like Michael knew we did it for him. She was pleased, and that was all that counted for me.

A couple of guys I knew from surrounding ranches stopped by. I didn't give them any encouragement for anything but friendship, but neighbor Bert Sampson made a habit of checking on me a couple of times a week. I admitted to myself that I enjoyed having a glass of iced tea on a warm afternoon with another young person. Bert understood my frustration of finding a new ranch hand, and agreed that most of the young men in the valley who didn't own their own land had moved to the cities for better paying jobs. Being responsible for all the decisions made on the ranch was something that I wished I could share. The world wasn't a fair place when a man who craved working on his own land, was taken away to brutal place. Evil people didn't deserve happiness, but Lee was good, more so than anyone I knew. I couldn't understand why he was taken and I was left with half a dream. Bert was a good listener, but I didn't want to lead him on, thinking we had a future.

Thanksgiving arrived without fanfare in the house. Admitting that I was spending too much time alone, I drove to Lakeview the next weekend, and picked up Fay on my way through Silver Lake. Ma was busy with their new expansion to the store. She suggested to Allen that a fabric department would be a good addition, along with associated supplies. She wanted help with ordering inventory, so Fay and I bent over catalogues, choosing fabrics, threads, patterns, trimming, and everything else we could think of for the department. Ma was beside herself with plans, and Allen indulged her every whim. Seeing her so happy, not worrying about money after all those hard years, and in a loving marriage, made me happy too.

While in Lakeview, I mentioned that I was going to place advertisements in the Bend and Lakeview newspapers for a ranch hand. Since Fort Rock Valley still lacked phone service, I picked a date when applicants could show up at the ranch for an interview. Ma doubted that I'd have more than one or two fellows come out, but it was worth a try.

My advertisement instructed applicants for the ranch position to arrive between noon and six o'clock on December 16th. The week had been unseasonably mild, pleasant enough that Sunny and I sat on the porch for coffee that morning. We took care of barnyard chores before I took a shower and washed my hair, certain that it was thicker than a few months earlier. My skin definitely had a healthier glow, and my figure had filled out.

After lunch, paperwork was my next chore that day. I'd been corresponding with a California rancher, who had a bull for sale that I was thinking of buying. I decided to make an offer for the bull and see where that would go. I answered Mona's last letter, excited about their new life in Los Angeles. She'd heard from Mabel, who decided to stay in the Army, which surprised us.

At 4 o'clock I was still alone, since no one arrived at the ranch about the job. Tired of being indoors, Sunny and I went to the barn where the horses patiently waited for attention. By the time I brushed Rusty and Socks, twilight was settling on the desert. I put the horses back into their stalls, and turned to walk through the barn and out the big doors.

A man was standing in the doorway, silhouetted against the lavender sky. I was startled, since I hadn't heard a car drive into the yard.

"I guess you're here about the job," I stammered, feeling very foolish. For a minute he didn't answer me.

Wait.

"Didn't you get my telegram?" the stranger asked.

What did he say?

"Ivy..."

Lee rushed towards me as I crumpled to the floor on my knees, sobbing into my hands. He swept me up in his arms, but I needed to see his face; my hands moved over his cheeks, mouth, nose...it was a thinner face, one that had seen hunger, cold, and hardship. But it was Lee's face!

"But, how...when...?" I asked, in between our frantic kissing.

"There's so much to tell you, Ivy. I've been dreaming about this moment for three years."

"Oh, Lee, I thought about you every day, but was afraid I wouldn't see you again," I sobbed.

"I'm here now, my darling, and would scoop you into my arms to carry you to the house, except I'm not in the best shape," he chuckled.

"Let me help, I'm good at this," as I slipped his arm over my shoulder. He was surprisingly light, even frail. I kept looking at Lee, afraid that my imagination had conjured him up. As we struggled into the house, Lee told me how he ran into Bert Sampson in Bend, who gave him a lift to our gate.

"Bert said you hadn't given up on me." I stopped to wrap my arms around Lee once more, and squeezed him most likely too hard. He brought his lips to mine and I felt the years being swept away.

When we stepped into the house, he commented that it looked

so different from what he remembered. I thought, "I have so much to tell him."

We sat on the edge of Ma's big bed, and I pulled off his new boots.

Lee asked, "Ivy, can we just lay here on the bed together? I need to feel you close and safe next to me."

"There's nothing I'd like better. You can tell me how you got out of Japan and when you got to the U.S." Neither of us understood why I wasn't notified when Lee was processed out of POW status. We talked far into the night, stopping long enough for a supper of sandwiches and milk.

Lee's story of survival exceeded anything I had heard. In Japan, he was moved around often the first two years, between camps that worked men to death. Finally he landed at a coal mine near Omuda. The conditions were brutal: lightly clothed in the severe winter, fed a scant bowl of rice or thin soup each day, and was submitted to beatings for the smallest infraction. But Lee managed to barely hang on. The prisoners heard about Germany's surrender, and soon the guards demanded a higher quota each day. When it wasn't met, some of the POW's were beaten to death, as an example of what could happen. By July the prisoners realized that their captors knew they were losing the war, and Lee thought they'd all be executed since they weren't needed. One evening some of the guards left their posts unmanned; Lee used the opportunity to escape. He told me that a poor family some distance from the mine found him hovering in their bath hut, sick, starving, and covered in coal dust. Instead of turning him in to the authorities, they nursed him back to health over the next four months. The news of Hiroshima's bombing, and Japan's surrender made just a small ripple in the remote village. When Lee's health improved enough so he could walk some distance, the family helped him reach another town where U.S. soldiers were processing the liberated prisoners.

By the middle of November, Lee was in Okinawa, and then sent to the U.S. He'd arrived in San Francisco just two weeks earlier and found out I was safe in Fort Rock. He sent me a telegram to meet him in Bend, but we'll never know what happened to it. He didn't want to see anyone else before reuniting with me, but when he arrived in Bend and I wasn't there, he located his parents. They told him I spent most of the war in the POW camp in Manila.

Lee wanted to know all about my internment, but I said it was nothing compared to his suffering. I explained how I'd used the charm bracelet to keep us alive. Lee grew somber with the thought I came so close to starving to death.

Lying side by side in the big bed with arms wrapped around each other, I told him that I'd decided to make the ranch my home, and asked if that was okay with him.

Lee said, "You are the best homecoming gift I could have, but living on the ranch comes a close second!" We laughed, talked, and slept, off and on all night. Once when he slept, I felt his body jerking, and his voice urgently warning someone in a whisper, "Hurry!"

In the early morning hours, I woke to find Lee standing at the bedroom window, and I saw the scars on his back and arms. He noticed that I was awake and immediately slid back under the blankets with me. We both were physically and emotionally shaken by our ordeals, but nothing could hold back our love for each other. As Lee moved his hands down my body, and I responded to his touch, I thought only of two young lovers just married in the rubble of war.

Over our first breakfast, Lee fished in his shirt pocket and presented me with a gold wedding band he purchased in San Francisco. Inside, an inscription read, "Ivy and Lee, Forever." Once he placed it on my finger, I never took it off for any reason.

Both Lee and I suffered from residual effects of imprisonment, but by late spring he could once again ride his horse out on the range. Lee's feet were always affected by cold weather, a result of suffering frostbite in the Japanese mines. Our children were never introduced to cooked rice, since just the smell made me sick. Our happiest day together occurred a few months after Lee returned, when the doctor in Silver Lake told me I was pregnant. My organs had been so stressed and deprived of nutrients during the war that I spent sleepless nights worrying about ever having a baby. Lee wanted to treat me like an invalid throughout my pregnancy, but I prevailed and helped with the chores right up until the last couple of weeks. Our son, David, was first, named for Lee's grandfather; followed by the two girls, Martha and Judith, for our mothers.

Lee used his engineering skills working for the county until he was sixty years old. I kept my hand in nursing as much as possible, but the ranch operations and children kept me mostly tied to home. Once our children were in college, I worked for the Silver Lake Clinic three days a week. Both Lee and I volunteered with the Fort Rock Fire Department Ambulance Service until Lee passed away from a heart attack when he was eighty years old. I almost let myself descend into a dark hole when I lost my closest friend, my dearest love; but my family expected me to hitch up my Levis and keep going.

Our life together was a fairytale; we loved and were loved with an intense respect for each other. Some bad winters wiped out the herds, and droughts took the crops; however, the ranch also grew right along with the children. The old house was replaced, but I still have a porch that faces the buttes. Every morning I drink my first cup of coffee while watching the range as the sun comes up."

# CHAPTER 22

RETURNING FROM HER SECOND TRIP IN FIVE years to Fort Rock, Oregon, Rosalie Evans and her husband, Ray, recalled David Johnson's words about his mother, Ivy.

He said, "Although we knew she had been an Army nurse, she never let on about the hardships that she, and Dad too, experienced during the war. Looking back, I now understand some of their habits and demands, like not being wasteful with food."

David and his sisters uncovered Ivy's handwritten memoir after she passed away. They were amazed at the details of their parents' lives in the Fort Rock Valley, and romance from high school to their reunion after WWII. Shocked at some of Ivy's revelations, the siblings marveled that she remembered so many important details. Since Ivy wrote the memoir after the missing photo album was returned just five years earlier, it seemed impossible that she could put into words the raw emotions felt so long ago. Rosalie remembered tracking down the album's owner after she bought it at a rummage sale in Portland, and visiting with the remarkable woman at her ranch.

Following his mother's passing, David contacted Rosalie about appraising a collection of Oregon books Ivy and Lee collected over the years. Rosalie and Ray owned Driftwood Books in Portland, specializing in rare and collectible items, and were often called to appraise estates. Ivy's family had already chosen the books they each wanted to keep. The remaining books would be auctioned after the appraisal, to help fund equipment for the local EMTs. After they finished cataloging the book collection, David asked if they'd look over the memoir. He wanted to publish it for their extended family members, and wondered if she'd help him find a good printing company in Portland. Rosalie eagerly accepted the manuscript; she knew the perfect company for the task.

As she and Ray drove Highway 31 towards Bend, the sun slipped below the horizon, giving each distant mountain a purple hue of differing shades.

"We have a long drive ahead of us, so why don't I read the memoir aloud while you drive," Rosalie said. Ray quickly agreed because he was as intrigued as she about Ivy's life.

After a sip from her water bottle, Rosalie began:

"Tracing my finger across the dusty window pane, I thought of all the house cleaning I could do if the well hadn't dried up."

# E P I L O G U E

SURROUNDED BY BOXES OF DISHES, LINENS, OF just plain living in one house, Rosalie complained to Ray that they should donate any household stuff they hadn't used in the last five years.

"If we haven't needed it for that long, let's not move it to the apartment," she begged. Ray was a pack-rat, and a hard-sell on disposing of his treasures.

"You don't mean my leftover house paints and power cords salvaged from old appliances, do you?" he asked.

"That's just the tip of the iceberg, Ray. The Las Vegas souvenirs from our vacation nine years ago can't even be donated, because no one wants them," Rosalie laughed.

The only undisputed collection was the boxes of books. Driftwood Books specialized in selling rare items, but the couple's private collection lined the halls of their house. With the upkeep on the house and yard becoming too much for Ray, they decided to sell the house and renovate the second floor above the shop. Having owned the building for twenty five years, they had used the upper floor only as storage for discarded shelving and holiday decorations between seasons. Renovations were underway to transform the area into the large, bright apartment they'd spent months designing. Both Ray and Rosalie loved the idea of being downtown near theaters and bistros. Many eateries and attractions were within walking distance, and their daughter, Penny, and her family, lived within ten minutes of the shop.

"Oh, look, Ray. Here's the book of Ivy's memoir. I always thought that Gorham's did a nice job on the printing and cover," Rosalie said, waving the book in his direction.

"I guess David Johnson's son has taken over the ranch by now. It's been a couple of years since he wrote of gradually turning the operation over to Bobby Lee," Ray recalled.

Rosalie perked up with an idea. "After we get the apartment finished and are moved in, why don't we take a day trip to Fort Rock? I'd love to see them again." Ray nodded, but was more interested in what he was sorting at the moment.

"Here's a little mini-cassette recorder I picked up at a garage sale sometime last winter. It came with this bag of tapes that are numbered in sequence. If it doesn't work, I'll let you toss it out," he offered. Right away it didn't work, but new batteries brought it to life. Ray loaded tape number one and pushed the "play" button.

A male voice, a smoker's voice, slowly began delivering a deliberate chronology, after a young female voice said, "Just talk normal, Grandpa."

Rosalie and Ray listened, captivated by the recording.

"I was born in 1925, to a…uh, farming family in Texas. We were poor, but that's not what I want to talk about. Ummm….in 1963 I got a job in Dallas, and moved my wife and two girls there that summer. I had a good job… keeping public parks mowed and clean. I was a good worker. But on November 22nd, I went to see President and Mrs. Kennedy in their motorcade, since it wasn't far from where I was working. I admired President Kennedy for his military service and what he was trying to do for our country. I…uh, stood on the grassy knoll, heard the shots and saw everything...even things that no one else saw. That's what I want to talk about."

The couple listened with their heads together over the tape player, occasionally looking at each other for the next twenty minutes. Finally the smoker's voice said, "That's all I have to say." Ray pushed the "stop" button.

"What have we got here, Rosalie?" he asked.

Almost in a whisper, she said. "What should we do?"

"Let's sleep on it tonight, Rosy girl." She nodded, and he tucked the cassette player back in the box under their coffee table.

"It might take two nights, Ray," Rosalie said as they turned out the lights.

# Acknowledgments

IN MARCH OF 2013, I READ AN obituary about the passing of Mildred Manning, the last survivor of WWII's "Angels of Bataan." Her personal story was amazing, and I had to know more about these nurses who came from small towns across the U.S. and enlisted in the Army Nurse Corps just prior to World War II.

Since this is a work of fiction, I had great latitude with my characters, but I tried to follow the chain of events during the Great Depression and World War II. Numerous accounts have been written about Bataan's Death March, prisoners of war, and the internees in Manila. I appreciate how painful it was for some survivors to put memories on paper. *We Band of Angels* by Elizabeth M. Norman holds a wealth of information about Army nurses sent to the Philippines. Also helpful were *Under the Samurai Sword* by C.M. Graham, and *Out in '45 If we're Still Alive* by Frieda Magnuson, both Central Oregon authors. None of the characters in *High Desert Angel* are real or based on any one person, except for Generals MacArthur, King and Wainwright.

The settlement of the High Desert of Central Oregon has inspired hundreds of books written by homesteaders and historians spanning 150 years. Raymond Hatton's *High Desert* and *Pioneer Homesteaders of the Fort Rock Valley*, plus Phil Brogan's *East of the Cascades*, helped with keeping the chronology of settlement on the desert correct.

Insights into hardships suffered by children during the Great Depression were gleaned from stories my own mother shared.

Descriptions of the quiet beauty of Oregon's High Desert come from my own experience. Stunning sunrises and sunsets, dark river canyons, blossom-laden hills, and a distant view of incredible peaks, provided me with all the adjectives I needed.